AFRICAN WRITERS SERIES
Editorial Adviser · Chinua Achebe

59

Rebel

AFRICAN WRITERS SERIES

Rebel

BEDIAKO ASARE

HEINEMANN
LONDON · NAIROBI · IBADAN

Heinemann Educational Books Ltd
48 Charles Street, London W1
PMB 5205, Ibadan · POB 25080, Nairobi

MELBOURNE   TORONTO   AUCKLAND
HONG KONG   SINGAPORE

SBN 435 90059-5

Illustrations by Taj Ahmed

Printed in Malta by St Paul's Press Ltd

Part One

1 Day came quickly to Pachanga. It came as a sudden burst of light which dramatically expelled the darkness. Ngurumo felt no sense of relief. He had spent a sleepless night, puzzled in mind and greatly distressed in his heart. His village was dying. It lay in the deep embrace of the jungle, isolated and unknown. A tribe of some hundreds of people were gradually starving. Absolutely isolated from the rest of the world, the people had learned to exploit their environment and adapt themselves to it. They had their own customs and religious concepts, albeit primitive, which they rigidly followed.

Pachanga was under the spell of a fetish cult. This took the form of the worship of gods of the river and the land. The gods were credited with the power to influence life on earth and were said to guide the destiny of the people. Even natural phenomena were attributed to the gods.

Mzee Matata was the intermediary between the living and the gods. A fat-skinned middle-aged man, he was regarded with awe and revered by all. Mzee Matata enjoyed tremendous prestige because it was believed he could set in motion the powers of the gods that could maim, destroy or make life abundant by a mere choice of incantation. He was also the soothsayer of the village and he alone could interpret omens. The exaggerated powers of the gods made the people submissive to the whims and caprice of Mzee Matata.

The people had sworn, at the risk of their lives, not to divulge secrets but always to obey faithfully the rules of the cult and defend its creed. They believed the gods controlled the destiny of the living and held the power of life and death. They were told to pay regular tribute to

3

the fetish priest and to offer sacrifices of living creatures to the gods at least once in twelve moons. Danger in any situation could be averted by invoking the gods. The punishment for major offences was death; pardon could only be granted through propitiation to the gods.

There had been the case of old Bishara. He refused to hand over to Mzee Matata the maize the fetish priest demanded from him as an offering to the gods.

'Mzee Matata,' Bishara said, bowing humbly before him, 'my wife is sick and she needs the maize. If she doesn't eat, she'll die.'

'Your wife won't die unless the gods say so.' Mzee Matata's manner was that of one who knew he was all-powerful and not to be defied. He sat aloof and disdainful but there was the petulance of anger about his mouth. He was not accustomed to opposition.

'But there are my children too,' Bishara protested. 'They——.'

'Enough!' Mzee Matata rose up, his flywhisk extended imperiously. 'Bring me the maize or your wife and children will die. Already, the gods are annoyed that you should dare oppose them.'

Bishara had not obeyed the fetish priest. Even the oldest man in the village could not remember anyone showing such defiance before. All said that Bishara's wife would die and perhaps also Bishara himself. And that was what happened. Bishara and his family all fell ill at the same time. They were lashed by an agony which caused them to writhe on the ground, whimpering, moaning and screaming.

When some people attempted to go to their aid, Mzee Matata forbade them.

'Bishara defied the gods that protect Pachanga,' he

4

said. 'The gods have decreed that Bishara and his family must die. Anyone who should so much as touch them may die also.'

The family's anguish filled the hearts of all who heard them with sympathy but, untended, Bishara, his wife and the children died. The same day their bodies were thrown into the river and the crocodiles devoured them in one twinkling of an eye. It was a sharp and painful lesson to everyone.

Ngurumo had not been as impressed as the others. In his young and questing mind, there were stirrings of doubt. Perhaps they might not have been there had he not seen Fundi, Mzee Matata's intimate companion and the one likely to be named by the fetish priest as his successor, sneaking into Bishara's hut carrying something in a pot. That was the day the family died and Ngurumo had pondered over it ever since. He could not dismiss the feeling that there was a close connection between that stealthy visit of Fundi and the death of the family. Bishara had returned from fishing to eat with his family and they had no sooner had their meal than pains started and all five of them were dying.

Ngurumo spoke about the matter to Seitu, his wife. 'I don't believe that the gods killed them,' he said. Seitu was shocked.

'You mustn't say such things,' she warned. 'You'll make Mzee Matata very angry.'

'I'm sure it was he who killed them,' Ngurumo replied. 'He had Bishara and his family poisoned.'

'But why?' Seitu asked.

'Because Bishara defied him.'

'Ngurumo, you mustn't say this.' Seitu's large eyes

were wide open with alarm. 'If you offend the gods they'll kill you as they killed Bishara.'

Ngurumo was chilled by his wife's reaction. If she did not believe him then nobody would. For their partnership had been strangely enough a happy one.

He had not chosen Seitu to be his wife. The choice, like all important decisions affecting the tribe, had been made by the gods. The parents of a youth of marriageable age approached Mzee Matata who consulted the gods. For it was they who decided who the girl should be and when the marriage should take place. When the parents had paid the fee required by the fetish priest, he would arrange his magical cowries and murmur incantations over them. Nobody understood what he mumbled. People chanted and drummed, until after a time, the priest would begin to weave his hands in the sand in front of him and fall into trance. Then he pronounced the name. In Ngurumo's case, it had been S – E – I – T – U.

Ngurumo was both relieved and pleased. She was the only girl he felt he could marry happily although he had not been too eager to marry at all. Nevertheless, parents had to be obeyed and the girl chosen by the gods was the one a youth had to marry.

Ngurumo had always liked Seitu. She was slender and graceful of movement with a happy disposition. She smiled readily and laughed easily. She had large expressive eyes. There was a yielding gentleness in her manner he found appealing. He was aware, too, of the ripeness of her figure. The aggressive thrust of her breasts and the narrowness of her waist attracted him. Her legs tapered from the smooth swell of her thighs to her slim feet. She wore a dress crudely made from

6

bark cloth and a number of bangles of beads and river shells around her neck, arms and legs.

Confident that she would make an agreeable companion, Ngurumo married her; and then came the astonishing revelation of love. He had not imagined that they could give each other so much joy. They loved tenderly. He was so filled with delight he felt he could live with her and be happy for ever.

Seitu too was happy with the marriage and she had as much reason to be pleased as he was. Ngurumo was tall and well built. His features were clearly defined. He had a high forehead with a broad face; his arms and shoulders were well muscled and his chest was deep. He could run untiringly for a long distance and he had distinguished himself in the hunt in which, like other youths, he was required to prove his manhood.

It was Ngurumo who had shown that cool courage which made him hold his hand until the lion he was stalking was only twenty footsteps away. By that time it was no longer running away. It had turned to face him. Many hunters of Pachanga had known this kind of situation and it had been too much for their nerves. They had thrown their spears too soon, either missing the lion altogether or only wounding it. After that there was not much chance. Some had succeeded in escaping by climbing a nearby tree but they had not been many. In some cases the lion had pounced on them, claws flashing and teeth gnashing, before they could even turn and run. Sometimes, the end had been instant death.

Ngurumo had not made that mistake. His nerves were so strong he could wait. However, his mouth had dried up, his body shook and there was fear in his heart. But his courage was equal to the terror which was prompting him to throw his spear. He had waited while the lion, roaring challengingly, ran at him. The urge to throw the spear at once was so strong that sweat burst all over his body. But he had resisted until the lion was making its leap. It was then that he threw the spear with all his strength. And, lo, the poisoned head, ground to a razor-like thinness, found its mark. It had plunged straight into the lion's throat. The animal stumbled in the air, twisting and writhing, and slumped to the ground almost at Ngurumo's feet. There was a cough from the fatally injured throat, a deep gurgling and blood rose as if from a fountain. Already its eyes were glazing. A few reflex twitchings in the leg, and the lion was dead. Ngurumo had proved his manhood.

Seitu was more than proud of such a bold and courageous man. He had shown himself to be a considerate and understanding lover too. Seitu had often heard some women talk about their husbands.

'A pig,' one of them had said. 'Ach! the things he does to me.'

'Throws me down on the floor,' another said. 'And he kicks me. My husband does not care for me.'

'Mine takes no notice of me at all,' said a third. 'He acts as if I'm not his wife.'

'Never leaves me alone,' said a fourth. 'I'm sick of him using me like a baboon.'

Ngurumo was not like any of these. He showed a deep interest in Seitu, talking to her a great deal. It was true that many of the things he often said worried and frightened her. He talked of ideas she had never heard of before. So she took them to be dangerous ideas.

'Mzee Matata,' he told her several times, 'pretends to protect the people. What he really does is to rob them. Look how short we are of food, but he doesn't go short. And he lives well.'

There were days he talked to her as a husband and a lover.

'You are good in the eyes,' he would say to her. 'Seitu, you are beautiful.'

She rejoiced to hear him say things of this sort. She was glad when he found her beautiful. It reassured her, because she knew that he was admired by so many people of the village. She had noticed how people looked at her sideways when she passed them. She used all her feminine wiles to make herself appealing.

But she soon found that he was not like other men. Experienced women had told her that it was easy to gain the passionate attention of the male.

'They're mad for their women,' she had been told, 'if you know how to excite them.'

'How?' she had asked. 'How does a woman make her husband want her?'

They chuckled at her innocence.

'It's so simple,' they told her. 'Press your mouth to his. Make sure your body touches his. Soon you'll have him wild with longing for you.'

But Ngurumo did not show pleasure when she approached him too openly. On the only occasion she flaunted herself at him, he stalked out of the hut, obviously greatly displeased. On his return, he explained to her that he did not wish her to make herself so obvious to him.

'You are my wife,' he reminded her. 'It is for the man to make the first move, not the woman. Talk to me whenever you wish. Say to me what you think is right – such things I shall not mind. I'll be glad to hear them. But let other relationships between us come as darkness and the morning sunlight which assuredly follows – naturally.'

*　　　*　　　*

Farming was the main occupation of the people. They also fished in the river, hunted or trapped wild game but these were done on a small scale.

Their method of cultivation was simple – all too simple. The land was tilled almost wholly with hoe and digging sticks. The ground was prepared for seed by cutting down trees and matted thickets. The strong heat of the tropical sun soon rendered the withered bushes fit to be consumed by fire. Farm work was done with the help of dependants for their common subsistence. At first, the crops had been reasonably healthy. But each succeeding crop became more meagre. Eventually, it became hardly worth harvesting. Preparing the ground for the seed, keeping down the hostile, obdurate weeds and gathering the crops – such as they were – taxed the people physically; they were arduous and exhausting exercises.

'There are easier ways of doing the work than the way we do it here,' Ngurumo told his wife.

'How can you know?' she asked.

'Didn't a great thing like a bird fall out of the skies on to our land one morning?'

Everyone had been terrified by the aeroplane. It was

10

beyond their understanding. True to tradition, Mzee Matata had offered an explanation.

'This strange thing with some peculiar creatures in it came purposely to destroy us, but the gods saved us by destroying them.' Mzee Matata had decreed that 'the devils from the sky' be burnt. And so a great bonfire was made and they were completely consumed.

The two creatures in the bird-like thing had not looked black like themselves and could not have been human beings. Their faces were hidden and their heads and ears were covered. Equally strange, they were encased from head to foot in a thick sort of outer skin. Some people said the thing had been roaring in the sky before it fell, and it was quite obvious even to the most simple minded that the creatures, whether they were human or not, could do something the people of Pachanga had never heard of. Ngurumo had thought a great deal about the two creatures and their marvellous artificial bird.

Where had they come from? How was it that they could fly? And why were they dressed so strangely? Besides, how did they make all the things they had with them? Ngurumo felt sure that people who could do such things did not grow their food in the way he and the people of Pachanga did.

As it was, they were working harder and harder for less and less food. The maize came up more and more thinly each time it was planted and the beans were ever fewer and smaller in their pods. Ngurumo did not know why this should be. And nobody in the village could offer a reasonable explanation. Of one thing Ngurumo was sure; they must be doing something wrong somewhere.

'What are we doing we shouldn't be doing?' Ngurumo asked the men working near him in the field one day.

They all stared at him blankly. They were doing what they had always done and as their forefathers had done for generations before them. To suggest that they were doing something wrongly was such an alien idea it was beyond their power of understanding.

'Wrong?' one of them shouted. 'Aren't we working as hard as ever? Didn't we sow at the right time and isn't this the right time to gather?'

'Yes,' Ngurumo indicated the thinly growing crops. 'But there's hardly anything to gather. This wasn't the way it used to be. Why do the crops grow so thinly now?'

They gave him their answer – the one he had expected.

'It's the gods,' they said. 'Didn't Mzee Matata tell us that the gods are angry with us and so they are forbidding the crops to grow well?'

'But why should the gods do that?' Ngurumo demanded. 'Why won't they let us have good crops? Haven't we sacrificed to them more than before? And didn't Mzee Matata promise that the crops would improve if we killed those goats and chickens and offered them to the gods as a sacrifice?'

No one answered. Instead they eyed Ngurumo nervously and glanced fearfully towards the sky. This, they knew, was dangerous talk. No one questioned the gods. To do so meant the most terrible punishment and, almost certainly, death. Mzee Matata had warned them of that often enough. The way Omari had died made them more terrified. He had been a strange youth. Some people even said he was possessed by evil spirits, judging by his manners. He had been in the habit of sneaking down to the river to watch the girls and women bathing there.

On one occasion, he startled everyone by riding a goat through the village, yelling at the top of his voice and frightening the children and old women. Such incidents were regarded as amusing, but it had not been amusing when he laughed very loudly at the time Mzee Matata was interceding with the gods. The sound had gushed forth suddenly in a hoarse manner, shattering the hushed silence. It was so unexpected that most people imagined they were dreaming. But swiftly the awful truth dawned on them. Omari was laughing.

Mzee Matata, quivering with rage, lifted a shaking hand and pointed a finger at the boy.

'The gods are offended,' he cried out. 'For this you shall die.'

Omari, overawed by the warning, had fallen silent. Everyone watched, as if expecting some bolt to hurtle from the sky to destroy Omari. And the fact that not even a cloud appeared to stain the blue sky did nothing to reassure them. The gods were merely exercising that cunning for which they had long been known. They would have their revenge in their own good time. All were quite sure that Omari would die.

And he did die. He was alone in his hut one day when a cobra appeared from beneath a mat. The youth, too petrified to move, stood still as if hypnotised until the snake was within two feet of him. Then he tried to kick out the snake and with a speed too quick for the eye to see, the cobra struck. A short while later, the cheerful, good-humoured, perhaps slightly unbalanced **Omari** was dead. The gods had taken their revenge.

But was it the gods who had acted against Omari? No one in the village was asking that question – no one except Ngurumo. The cobra made him suspicious. Had Omari dropped dead, without any obvious physical action or without reason, Ngurumo would have been as convinced as the rest that the gods had killed the youth. In this case it was a cobra that brought about his death. There was something in the situation that did not convince Ngurumo. Supposing Mzee Matata or his aides had secreted the cobra in Omari's hut? This thought made him tingle with excitement.

2   The day's work was over, and after dinner Ngurumo and his wife retired to bed. It was earlier than usual. The moon did not shine that night. Seitu stirred in her sleep and flung out a careless hand. It came to rest lying across Ngurumo's stomach. The contact caused him to look at her. She was young, innocent and lovely. For a moment he lost the trail of the ideas revolving in his mind.

Then his thoughts switched on to the fate of the people of the village. Warmth spread from his stomach into his chest. It was not the first time he had felt like this. The pathetic situation had always outraged him. He had nothing with which to compare it. But there

14

burned in him the unquenchable belief that things could be better – much better.

Ngurumo was persuaded of this by the uncultivated land that lay to the east of the village. It was a rich land on which fat crops would grow. No one else occupied it or claimed it. For all the people of Pachanga were aware, they were the only human beings under the sun unless, of course, the two creatures who dropped down from the sky some moons ago had been human beings.

The isolation of the people was due to several factors. Although they did not know it, they lived on one part of a huge pear-shaped island off the coast of Africa. It saddled the Equator and lay in the tropical zone. The island tapered in the south to half of its width. The central feature was a mountainous range almost triangular in shape enclosing Pachanga. It was covered by dense, tall, tropical forest. In the olden days, it had been said that it was the abode of evil spirits and even now no one wished to visit that part of the island.

Pachanga itself was almost invisible from the air. The huts were huddled together along narrow, dark and filthy lanes and enjoyed the protection of the tall, close-growing trees. The buildings were depressingly primitive. The framework was of nothing more substantial than reeds and these were tied together with the stems of the creeping plant and plastered with mud. The roofs were either thatch made from the fronds of palm trees which grew profusely nearby, or they were made of a certain type of tall grass stuck together to form thick, broad sheets. The huts often had only one aperture, a doorway. The outer walls of some of them were made to look picturesque with life-like frescoes of people, animals and fish.

The only building which could lay claim to distinction was that of Mzee Matata who ruled the people as his ancestors had ruled them in the past. This dwelling stood a little apart on a hillside. It was built with mud and studded with stones. It suggested that the people might be imbued with some degree of architectural skill as it had a symmetrical dome which served as a sort of a watch tower from which Mzee Matata could look upon all the huts in the village. There was also a large ceremonial courtyard where decrees were issued, pronouncements made and where the fetish priest and ruler deigned to meet his people.

Sanitation in the village was deplorable. People simply tossed their refuse out of their huts, and thus unwittingly turned every inch of trodden land into a breeding ground for a whole catalogue of highly dangerous diseases.

Behind each hut was a small stretch of garden. There were grown legumes, tubers and bananas to supplement the basic diet of maize. The joints of the branches of some of these plants were hollow enough to store rain water and so provide breeding places for mosquitoes, flies, tsetses and other disease-carrying insects.

A single roadway divided the village. There was an astonishing tradition that the people on one side of the road descended from the sky, while those on the opposite side had emerged from the heart of the earth. The belief had been handed down by word of mouth from generation to generation and it had resulted in there being two different clans in Pachanga. But all acknowledged the one ruler – Mzee Matata.

The people on both sides of the road were in danger. Ngurumo had seen the problem assuming an increasing urgency for some time. He had watched the people becoming leaner and he had been greatly shaken by the outbreak of diseases, even though the visitations were not new. There had been dreadful epidemics in the past and more than a quarter of the people had been killed; amongst them had been Ngurumo's mother. His parents had been taken ill together. He had been with them, watching helplessly as the disease ravaged them. His mother talked wildly at the height of the fever and Mzee Matata explained that evil spirits had possessed her. The fetish priest muttered strange words to drive them away; then he gave both Ngurumo's parents herbal mixtures. But neither magic nor medicine could help Ngurumo's mother and she died within two days.

That made Ngurumo wonder why Mzee Matata claimed to be so powerful. He could not persuade the gods to come to the rescue of the people. More than once Ngurumo had asked why. And Mzee Matata was ready with his answer.

'The gods are exceedingly angry with you,' he said. 'It's essential to regain their goodwill.'

No one asked how this was to be done. Not only was it an offence to interrupt Mzee Matata when he was speaking, but all knew the answer before he uttered it.

'The gods require sacrifices of goats and chickens. Ten goats and one hundred chickens. They have to be brought to the shrine by tomorrow when the sun is at its height.'

His finger would be pointed at each man in turn.

'You'll bring a goat. And you'll bring a chicken.'

There was no reason offered as to why one man should bring a goat and the other a chicken. The arbitrary levies were accepted without protest but Ngurumo felt a surge of resentment when the fetish priest pointed at him and said, 'You'll bring a goat,' He felt like shouting out, 'No, no, that's too much!' But prudence made him keep quiet.

That evening, alone in his hut with Seitu, he gave vent to his feelings.

'The people are underfed,' he said. 'To destroy so many chickens and goats means still less for the people to eat. If the gods wish the people well, they would have saved them from the illness which killed so many of them.'

'Hush – oh, hush!' Seitu placed a hand over his mouth. 'If anyone should hear you and report what you have said to Mzee Matata, he would appeal to the gods to have you destroyed.'

Gently but firmly he removed her hand from his mouth.

'And if the gods paid him no more heed than when he exhorted them to spare the people, then I should have nothing to fear.'

'No, no! You mustn't speak like that. Mzee Matata himself will kill you.'

'Ah – ha! So you know that.' He reached out a hand and patted her shoulder approvingly. 'I know you've more wits than some of the girls.'

'Speak discreetly,' she warned. 'Mzee Matata has great powers.'

'Why do you say that?'

'Because nothing happens in the village that he doesn't hear about. Who tells him these things if not the gods?'

'Those who live to gain by telling lies.'

'You mean informers!'

'Of course. Fundi is one of them. He's all the time prowling between the huts and creeping up on gossiping men and women.'

'But why should he do that?'

'For rewards. Look at the favourable treatment he received when he grew weary of his wife.'

'His wife died,' Seitu sighed.

'She was murdered,' Ngurumo corrected. 'And by Fundi.'

'How do you know this?' Seitu looked up, startled.

'Because I went to the Hut of the Dead on the day that she died.'

'But no one is allowed to go there!' Seitu said in disbelief.

Ngurumo rose. Then he sauntered from the hut. He came back after having made sure that nobody was around eavesdropping.

'No one is there,' he chuckled. 'But I had to make sure.' He reseated himself on the floor close to his wife. 'You remember that Mzee Matata announced that Fundi's wife died of the sickness that is all heat?'

Seitu nodded.

'Well, I felt there was something fishy about it and I made it my business to see whether I was right. So I went to the Hut of the Dead where she was laid awaiting her funeral the following day. D'you know what I saw?'

'No, tell me more,' she replied.

'Her throat was cut from ear to ear.' Ngurumo told his wife in a whispering tone.

'Who could have done such a dastardly thing?' Seitu gasped with horror.

'Who else but her husband?'

'But why? After all Fundi's wife was a good worker. She did her best for the husband and the children.'

'Yes she did. But she was showing signs of old age. She was no longer as beautiful as before. Her body was beginning to sag. Besides, Fundi had his eyes on someone else.'

'Abiba?'

'Yes. She was his wife's closest friend, as you know, and he had been wanting her for some time. Once his wife came upon them hiding in some bushes by the river.'

'And you think that Mzee Matata had Fundi's wife murdered?'

'Of that I'm not sure but he gave Fundi his protection. No one had heard that the woman was ill. In fact on the morning of the day she died she was hale and sound. Then, just before nightfall, Fundi announced that his wife was dead, killed by the hot sickness. As he had his eyes on Abiba, I knew he had reason to want his wife dead. Why was she hurried to the Hut of the Dead before anyone had seen her?'

Seitu looked perplexed. 'Don't implicate Mzee Matata,' she warned. 'He'll kill you if you do that.'

'Something has to be done,' said Ngurumo firmly.

'No, no! You and I are happy. I don't want people to go against you. They're all afraid of Mzee Matata. You'll be destroyed before you could do anything.'

'That could be,' Ngurumo agreed. 'But I've no choice.'

'Why have you no choice?'

'Because all the people of the village will perish unless some one saves them. And who else is there if I don't do it?'

The answer puzzled Seitu. Her good-natured features were drawn together in a worried frown.

'What's this danger you speak of?' she asked.

'It's clear. People must have food. And there's less and less to gather at each succeeding harvest. There can be only one end to this – we shall all slowly starve to death. Even now illness visits us.'

'That's because we're offending the gods. Mzee Matata says they're angry with us.'

'Why should they be angry with us and for how long?' Ngurumo demanded. 'What are we doing now that we haven't done always and always?'

Seitu began to scratch her head as she pondered her reply.

'It's true that someone has murdered Fundi's wife,' Ngurumo said, 'but Mzee Matata hasn't said that the murder has angered the gods. Nothing has been done about the killing. What have the people done then that has offended the gods?'

Seitu did not say a word. Apparently she understood her husband now.

'We've our days to honour the gods. We sacrifice to them. The virgins dance naked in their honour. We neglect nothing. Still the gods are angry with us. We've sacrificed more than usual. Didn't we make the special sacrifice recently at the command of the fetish priest? What did we achieve from that? We destroyed the precious animals for nothing.'

'What can you do about that?' Seitu asked her husband.

'That I don't know yet. But I mean to do something,' he replied.

Since then, Ngurumo had been scheming hard. He

21

knew it would be dangerous for him to defy Mzee Matata. He was aware, too, that he could expect little help from anyone in the village. Some of them would be hostile to him. There could be severe penalties for daring to defy the gods. Ngurumo knew too that Mzee Matata would not limit his vengeance to him alone. He would certainly direct his wrath against Seitu also. It was this which had caused Ngurumo to stay his hand. But that thought was fast losing its restraining influence. The villagers were in real danger of perishing. Yet they persisted in their follies to the gods and admiration of Mzee Matata.

Ngurumo looked again at Seitu. She aroused in him a deep tenderness. Any pain she might suffer would cause him an almost unbearable anguish. On the other hand his people were doomed. The latest harvest was the worst yet. The people, who had been living more and more on fish from the two rivers which cut across the land were finding it harder to catch anything worth while. The rivers had been robbed of the fish which had remained constant for as long as anyone could remember.

The memory of the people went far, far back. The aged gave information to the young ones. Before adolescence children had been told of the history of Pachanga, its beliefs and folklore. Much was said of the past. There had been a fire on one occasion, but the fetish priest ruling at the time had persuaded the gods to blow the flames away from the village. The people were saved. A long, long time ago, a terrible flood ravaged about a third of the village. The Kankan river, swollen by torrential rains, broke its banks and swept through the village causing damage to life and property. Many people and domestic animals were drown-ed. Several huts were washed away and crops were destroyed. It was believed by those who survived that it was the gods which saved them.

They had not blamed the gods for the untold damage done. As usual, they were told to offer sacrifices in thanksgiving to the gods.

This was the attitude of the people towards disaster. They were inclined to accept everything fatalistically. The gods had every right to be capricious and even malicious. If they wished to destroy, no one should complain against them. To complain, as the fetish priest never wearied of pointing out, was to incur the wrath and spite of the gods.

Ngurumo did not accept this belief. Disaster was overtaking his people. And he was sure that there was no need for it. Suddenly, his mind was made up. He would challenge the fetish priest. He would pit himself against Mzee Matata.

3   Ngurumo eased himself from his wife and rose to his feet. Soon the village would be astir and he wished to walk about and refresh his mind before noise and movements disturbed his peace. His gaze lingered for awhile on the still sleeping Seitu. She was lovely, he said to himself. He wanted her to have a good and a long life. Unless something was done now she would soon famish like the rest of the people.

Ngurumo turned away from her and stepped out of the hut. There was as yet only a mild warmth in the sunshine and it soothed his skin in a way that gave him a feeling of satisfaction. He stepped carefully to avoid the worst of the refuse that clustered the narrow lanes. Already flies were buzzing in the flickering morning light and swarming around the stinking litter.

His walk took him beyond the village and over the cultivated land which had such a barren look about it. Almost all the crops had been gathered. What remained reminded Ngurumo of an old man's beard. It was sparse and straggly and appeared to be dying. He stopped to look at the remains, with his left hand firm on his hip and his right palm supporting his chin. His eyes lingered on the ungathered crops across the fields.

He could remember when this same plot gave fat crops, the ripening grains hissing and whispering in the wind. As a boy, he had watched the rich green crops grow into equally rich golden harvest. There had been abundance then. He wondered what had brought about this change. Were the gods really angry with the people and so were denying them the food they needed to live? If so, why? That was the question he had asked himself so often. Why? Why? Why? He had failed to find the answer. Perhaps the gods were spiteful and filled with malice. Perhaps they delighted in tormenting the people who often paid them homage and offered them sacrifices. The gods must be very strange. Was not every possible effort made to gain their favours and good graces? He found himself recalling the day they made the big sacrifice of goats and chickens.

24

The unfortunate creatures were slaughtered at the ceremonial ground in front of Mzee Matata's house according to long-standing practice. First the chickens were taken by the fetish priest and their heads were severed from their bodies by a single stroke of a very sharp knife. The sight of the blood and the smell as it filled the air had infected the people watching the ceremony with an emotion Ngurumo could not describe.

Then came the killing of the goats. They were all males, young and strong. Immediately they caught the smell of blood, they became frightened. They began to bleat in alarm and they struggled to escape. They leapt and plunged as they tried to free themselves from the stakes to which they were tethered.

The method of slaying them was particularly cruel. In turn, each was laid on the sacrificial stone. The legs were tied fast to a separate stake driven deep into the ground. And then Mzee Matata took a knife and opened the belly of the goat. The hapless animal set up a wailing and howling that alarmed everybody. Ngurumo, distressed by the spectacle, had looked away. It was a sight he was unable to forget.

He had not resented the goats being sacrificed because one of them was his, although, having fed it for moons without any return, it had been taken from him and destroyed just as it was ready to become the father of many kids. He could not understand how it was that the people could watch the painful killings without reaction. It stirred in him a thought which frightened him.

'How do the gods feel when they see a helpless animal having its belly ripped open? Does it satisfy them? If so, then out of gratitude they should have rewarded us with a big harvest. Instead, the crops have been hardly worth gathering.'

Sacrifice, by the use of a knife that caused an animal to die in agony, was traditional. In the past it had been people who died like that. According to stories, it had been the custom before sowing time to sacrifice a virgin to ensure that the crops flourished. This custom was abandoned when it was seen that it was leading to a shortage of women. Men had begun to complain that there were not sufficient wives for all of them. The sacrifice of the virgin ceased. Now it was chickens and animals.

Having crossed the land which had been set aside for cultivation, Ngurumo found himself approaching the river. It was wide and shallow. He had spent many happy moments beside it and in it. There were nights when the reflection from the moon's rays made the surface of the water sparkle like silver. As a boy, he had swam and bathed in it almost daily. Like others, he still immersed himself in the cool water every other day or so. He also set traps made of sisal and when he was lucky, he caught flounders, mud-fish and trout.

He waded to his traps. He was the richer by only one small flounder. Not so long ago he would have been compelled to throw this back into the river, but the shortage of food had caused Mzee Matata to relax this rule.

Ngurumo did not return to the village from there. He followed a winding track through the forest. He marvelled at the majesty of the trees which soared until it seemed that their branches brushed against the sky. They grew close together and beneath their intertwining twigs and branches flourished a rich variety of bushes and creeping plants. As he moved along he caught glimpses of squawking parrots and monkeys jumping merrily from tree to tree.

The jungle provided shelter for lions, tigers, zebras, giraffes, and buffalos. Elephants too were there in numbers, and thousands of rodents. The jungle contained a large number of pythons and there were many cobras and mambas as well as other poisonous snakes.

Ngurumo knew that there was little to fear from the animals of the jungle. They rarely attacked men and women unless they were provoked. Nature has provided them with ample food and they were content to live on their natural prey. But there was the risk of being lost. More than once people had missed the usual tracks and they had never been seen again or had been found only after they had died.

There was danger in the vast spread forest. Ngurumo was struck by the eerie atmosphere. There were noises which indicated that killing and being killed was an inescapable law of the jungle. There were grunts, sudden screams, snarlings, scurryings and flurries.

He came across a pride of lions devouring their kill. He took great care not to disturb the feeding animals. From his earliest days he had been warned that animals satisfying their hunger might misunderstand the presence of a human being and attack before he had the chance to escape.

Ngurumo had not ventured deep into the jungle. He was passing through the narrow band of forest which separated the village from that piece of land about which he had been thinking so much of late. He soon broke out of the line of trees and undergrowth. There it lay before him, a vast stretch of richly growing grass.

He saw this fertile reach of territory as the answer to the problems of his people. Soil that would support grass of such richness would also produce fat crops. For some time he glanced about in satisfaction at the wind-stirred grass. It rose shoulder high and it was a rich emerald. It would provide excellent pasture for many herds of cattle. But the people had never been too keen on large-scale breeding. This was understandable. The ground they cultivated was needed to grow food for themselves. There was little to spare for animals. So the people kept only a few of them.

Here large herds of cattle could graze and the grass would replace itself almost as quickly as it was eaten. It would be possible to do more than grow maize. Bananas, tubers, beans and many other kinds of vegetables would grow well on the land. Here was abundance. Here was life-giving land. And here was a magnificent scenery too. Away to the north rose mountains. They seemed to rise sheer out of the earth to mist-crowned peaks. On the tops of those mountains there gleamed a wonderful whiteness at one time of the year. The whiteness when touched by the sun became bright and melted, water running down the slopes.

'Yes,' Ngurumo began to soliloquise, 'this is where my people must live. This is where they can thrive. Here they can begin again. And life will take on a new meaning.'

The more he thought about it, the more he became convinced that he had the solution to his people's problems firmly in his grasp. Of course he would have to persuade them to act on his idea but he was sure he would have little or no difficulty. He would tell them of his plans and they too would be enthusiastic about such a move. He would take some of the men to the spot and explain to them all that he had in mind. He felt a thrill of jubilation. He had found the gateway to a new life for his people. Seitu would enjoy living here. She would see her children grow up strong and well nourished.

He made his way back home through the forest feeling so light of heart that he hummed softly a popular traditional song. He came out of the forest at the point where he had first entered it, near the Kankan river. The river, like the land, was the abode of the gods.

Near it was a shrine containing an altar on which were placed offerings. The shrine was shabbily constructed and in a state of disrepair. Ngurumo did not go near it. He knew that inside it were a number of wooden idols blackened by the blood of animals spilled on to them as libation. There was also an elephant's skull. In the foreground was a large earthenware pot containing what was regarded as holy water which had the power to drive away evil spirits. Worshippers washed their faces, hands and feet with the water before they entered the shrine. Virgins filled the pot with water from the Kankan river each day and the fetish priest uttered those words over it which gave it its sacred and consecrated quality.

Reaching home, he found that the villagers were already beginning their day. Fires were being lit and the meagre morning meals were being cooked. In his own hut, he found Seitu near to panic.

'Oh! Ngurumo,' she cried out. 'I was terrified when I found you weren't here.'

29

'I didn't want to wake you up when I left the hut,' he said.

'Where have you been?'

'To look at the place where we can all begin to live again.'

Her troubled look gave way to one of bewilderment.

'Beyond the wide belt of forest,' he explained, 'where the grass grows tall, thick and very green. The soil there springs with life – life for our people and for our children.'

'But will Mzee Matata agree to go there?'

'Why shouldn't he?'

She would not say why the fetish priest would reject the idea, but she was convinced that he would. She felt the depression that comes from forebodings of evil.

'Certainly, you'll like living there,' Ngurumo said. 'It's open ground. The sun shines right on to it.'

'I'm happy anywhere with you,' she said but added quickly, 'I'm a bit worried. You're too bold and daring. I know and appreciate your strength as a man. I'm proud of your courage. But a man can be over bold. And the gods don't like defiance.'

'I'm not defying the gods,' he replied. 'When have they ever said that we mustn't live on new land?'

She could not answer but she was still far from satisfied.

'Come,' Ngurumo said, 'let's eat. Then I'll take some men of wisdom and knowledge to view the land where we can live in happiness and prosperity.'

Seitu was a good cook but she could not make a satisfying meal with what was available. The maize was boiled perfectly. It was served with a little chicken but it failed to satisfy Ngurumo's appetite. He did not complain, knowing that his wife had done her best.

Because there was not very much to do that day, about twelve men agreed to go with Ngurumo to look at the vast spread of virgin land.

'Yes, it's good,' they said in unison. 'It's very good.'

'Everything is here,' Ngurumo was at pains to point out. 'The Kankan river is just nearby and there's also a stream that crosses the land.' He pointed to it.

'There's plenty of wood, and sisal is available. We have all the materials we need to build for ourselves new houses. Here we'll no longer have to sweat and strive hard to gain food which barely keeps us alive. Here there'll be plenty of everything for everybody.'

'Yes, yes, it's better here,' they conceded.

'Then let's make preparations to move here without delay,' Ngurumo said.

'Let's do that as soon as possible,' they all agreed.

They went back to Pachanga well pleased with all that they had seen. Rejoining his wife, Ngurumo told her elatedly, 'they're as eager to go there as I am. What did I tell you, girl of my heart? To see the land is to covet it and decide to have it.'

'What does Mzee Matata say?' Seitu asked.

'I don't know what he says,' replied Ngurumo. 'In any case, what can he say if the people agree to move?'

'Whatever he says, you may be sure that the people will obey him. No matter how desirous they may be of the land, they'll obey their fetish priest and ruler.'

Ngurumo knew it could be so. But he was hopeful. Surely good sense would prevail. After all, the people were facing the stark reality of the situation – they must move or perish. They knew this too well.

The mid-day meal was over. People took shelter

from the heat of the hot sun in their huts. They lay stretched on mats relaxing or dozing. The village turned quiet during the hours of siesta. However, the period of rest was barely over when the silence was unexpectedly disturbed by the beating of a drum.

'People of Pachanga,' a voice proclaimed, 'Mzee Matata orders every man and woman to go to the sacred ground before his house. You are all to go there at once.'

Instantly, the whole village began to buzz with chatter as people speculated what the meeting was about. Seitu turned pale. She held Ngurumo by the arm, and gazed into his eyes. There was a taut silence and then with bated breath she said, 'I'm afraid.'

'There's no reason to be afraid,' he blurted. 'Mzee Matata has heard of the wishes of the people. He's calling us before him to confirm that we're to move to the fertile land.'

Seitu did not share his optimism. Silently she followed him into the open. The narrow lanes were filled with people obeying the summons. Soon all the men and women of the village were standing in a wide arc. They were no longer talking; they were silent and anxiously waiting for their ruler to appear and speak.

It was not Mzee Matata's way to come out to them at once. Even when all the people were obviously present and in place, he still kept them waiting. Only after he had impressed upon them that it was their duty to wait upon his good pleasure did he deign to appear. He emerged from the house at last, his personal servant walking behind him and carrying the bunch of ostrich feathers, the symbol of the fetish priest's divine authority.

Mzee Matata presented an impressive picture. His full body was heavily decorated. He wore charms and talismans of magical significance. Around his neck, arms and ankles were bands of closely knit leaves. On his body he wore a loose raffia skirt. The much befeathered headress stood in stiff magnificence upon his bare head. He approached the stone of sacrifice at a slow, regal pace. Those near enough to see his features in detail saw that he looked grim and angry.

Reaching the stone, he halted. He turned round looking sullen but with an air of importance and at the same time shaking his head in anger. His whole manner was one of contempt for the people. His every movement and gesture was designed to impress.

He raised his right arm with dramatic suddenness and then cleared his throat. The place was silent.

'Countrymen,' he began, his voice loud and threatening, 'I've heard evil information concerning some of you. You wish to leave the land set aside for you by the gods and live elsewhere. This the gods forbid. Any man or woman who goes to the Land of the East will surely die.'

Fear gripped their hearts.

'The one who has sown this dangerous idea amongst you is Ngurumo,' Mzee Matata said, bringing his arm round until he was pointing at Ngurumo. He gestured imperiously.

'Step forward,' the fetish priest commanded.

Seitu began to shake violently. Ngurumo squeezed her arm reassuringly before he left his place. All eyes were turned on him as he advanced towards the centre. He tried not to hurry his pace and he strove hard not to betray his nervousness. He came to a halt some two arms-lengths in front of Mzee Matata. As custom demanded, he bowed three times and then straightened up. Mzee Matata looked scornfully at him right in the face. Ngurumo saw in the black depths of the fetish priest's eyes a cold and deadly rage.

'So you're the ignorant youth who presumes to be wiser than the gods,' Mzee Matata said. His voice grew harsh and gruff. 'You're the one who wants nothing less than to see the whole people move to another dwelling place. Did you consult the wishes of the gods before you came to this decision?'

Ngurumo felt the heat of anger gripping his stomach. He knew well that he had been called out in order to be humiliated and ridiculed. He had not consulted the gods, for they could only be approached through the fetish priest.

'You know I haven't approached the gods,' he replied rather boldly.

'Then you presume to be wiser than they are?'

'No. I simply felt that the gods would approve of what's so obviously good.'

The fetish priest's face coloured angrily.

'The gods don't wish the people to move,' he said. 'The land you think we should take over is for the devil and the gods will punish most severely anyone who goes to live on it.'

Ngurumo took a deep breath. He knew that he had already taken a step which was likely to result in his undoing. He had done so feeling that Mzee Matata would agree to the step as a wise one. Now he realised he should have known that the fetish priest would be deeply offended by what he had done. Ngurumo thought that with all the people around, he had better put his views across. If he did not say it now, they would not hear him again for they would be too afraid to listen to him now that the idea had been condemned. He decided to speak out for he would never again have such a chance.

'Mzee Matata,' he said in a loud, clear voice, 'I feel that the gods prompted my idea.'

He heard the fetish priest's sharp intake of breath. This was almost open rebellion.

'In fact,' Ngurumo went on, trying to prevent his voice from shaking, 'the gods have spoken to me a great deal for some days. They've warned me that either the people should move or they will perish.'

Murmur went up from the assembled people. Whether it signified that they agreed with him or they were astonished at his temerity in arguing with Mzee Matata, he did not know. He had no choice but to carry on.

'We can't survive here any longer. Almost all the fish have been taken from this stretch of the river. The land yields less and less food. Our animals are growing steadily thinner and the people are becoming more and more hungry.'

There was another murmur from the assembly.

'Silence!' Mzee Matata commanded in a voice shaking with rage. 'We know that the crops aren't what they should be. Our stomachs, not the gods, tell us that. But this is because the gods are displeased with us. They're angry and they won't give us abundant food until they're appeased.'

'If this is the case,' said Ngurumo, 'how are we to appease them? Didn't we make a large sacrifice to them only two moons ago? Did the chickens and goats gain their favour? They can't have, for the harvest this time is smaller than ever before.'

'Well, that's so,' said Mzee Matata, 'but it seems the gods are demanding a very special sacrifice.'

A sudden burst of '*e-e-e-h-h-h*' rose from among the assembled people followed by a mock laugh in a quiet, suppressed manner.

'Yes,' said the fetish priest, his face still grave, 'a most special sacrifice.'

'What's it to be this time?' Ngurumo asked. 'If we kill any more goats and chickens, we shall have even less to eat.'

'I can't answer your question now,' said Mzee Matata. 'The gods have only told me that a special sacrifice is needed. In their own good time they'll tell me what they need. Meanwhile, let there be no misgivings about the wishes of the gods. We're to remain in Pachanga where we have lived for so long. To forsake the land sacred to our forefathers would mean death for every individual who leaves.'

He gestured, indicating that the meeting was over.

The fetish priest felt uneasy. If Ngurumo succeeded in moving the people, it would mean the end of the cult which from time immemorial had wielded considerable influence in the village. It would also mean the end of his easy means of earning a livelihood. In his mind a plot was evolving. Ngurumo must die.

From the position where he stood facing the crowd, Ngurumo went back to Seitu. She had been greatly disturbed by what had happened. They walked along together, but she said nothing until they reached the privacy of their hut. She had not expected her husband would behave the way he did at the meeting.

'Ngurumo, I'm frightened,' she told him as tears flooded her eyes. 'You've greatly angered Mzee Matata and he'll not forgive you.'

'I spoke the truth, Seitu,' he said. 'You know I did.'

'Yes, I know, but what good has it done? You should have known that Mzee Matata would say nay to your ideas.'

'I thought for the sake of the people, he wouldn't. If he persists in compelling the people to stay here, all of us, including Mzee Matata himself will starve to death.'

Friends began to worry for Ngurumo. They remembered what had happened to Bishara and Omari. They appealed to him to change his mind before it was too late. Every day someone pleaded with him to drop his scheme. His own father became restless fearing the outcome of Ngurumo's stand. It could even mean the total extinction of the whole family by the powerful gods. But Ngurumo paid no heed to anybody. His obstinacy rather hardened. He even forgot that he had sworn an oath of allegiance to obey the gods through thick and thin. There was a strong urge in him to go ahead with his plans.

'Come what may,' was his retort to all those who sought to plead with him.

Neighbours began to despise him. They would neither greet him nor reply to him. Some treated him like an outcast. There was no doubt in people's minds that he was going to die.

One evening, while Ngurumo and Seitu were talking, the opening in the hut darkened and his father entered.

'Ngurumo!' the old man exclaimed. For a moment, he looked at his son, shaking with fear. 'What's wrong with you?' he asked.

37

'I've done what I think is right,' said Ngurumo.

'What you've done has so angered the gods that you'll die,' his father's voice gruff with annoyance. 'How dare you offend Mzee Matata in such a way? He's bound to call upon the gods to punish you.'

'My father,' Ngurumo shouted back, 'if we're to survive, we must move. The fertile land that awaits us lies to the east.'

'The gods have said that the Land of the East isn't for us and so it can never be ours. You would be wise to offer Mzee Matata some of your chickens as a token that you're sorry. Then tell him that you've given up your ideas which you now see to be wrong.'

Ngurumo was shocked by the suggestion.

'I'm not wrong,' he protested.

But the old man was sure his son was very wrong.

'The gods will punish you,' he warned. 'You'll be sorry you've acted in this way. Make your peace with Mzee Matata before it's too late.'

And turning, he left the hut.

'Your father is right,' Seitu said. 'No good can come from what you've done.'

'I can't say that I'm wrong when I know that I'm right,' Ngurumo insisted.

'Listen to me,' his wife pleaded. 'You must listen to me. If you oppose Mzee Matata he'll kill you. You know he will.'

This was quite probable. Never had the fetish priest been so opposed. His word was law. He was not to be challenged.

'He'll find some means of killing you,' Seitu repeated.

'Yes, you may be right.'

Ngurumo faced the fate all rebels against absolute power had always faced. In challenging Mzee Matata, he had virtually signed his own death warrant.

'Do as your father said. Make your peace with Mzee Matata. Do it for my sake, Ngurumo, if not for your own,' she begged him on her knees.

'I'll think it over,' he replied, sinking down on to the stool nearby. 'There's one thing I can do,' he said. 'I'll go away from here and live on the fertile Land of the East.'

Seitu eyed him in a startled silence.

'Would you go with me?' he asked her.

Seitu did not answer him. Rather she put another question. 'Don't you think we shall be alone there?'

'At first, yes. But others may follow later. In any case, we shall have plenty to eat. If we stay here, we'll surely die of starvation. If we go away, we shall be able to live free of fear.'

Seitu was silent.

'It's my only chance,' he grinned. 'If I've offended Mzee Matata as deeply as I think, what guarantee is there that he'll forgive me?'

'But if the gods have forbidden us to go as he says they have, won't they be very angry with us and destroy us no matter where we may go?'

'The gods are angry with us even here. How do we know that they aren't trying to goad us into starting a new life elsewhere?'

'Mzee Matata says that this ground is sacred to them and that they've hallowed it as ours for ever. How can they want us to go away?'

'We must, we must,' Ngurumo said repeatedly. 'I

feel it in my heart and soul. There's nothing more we can do.'

He took Seitu's hand.

'I don't wish to place you in danger of any sort but if you won't go with me, then I'll have to go alone.'

'So you want to leave me behind?' Seitu was appalled.

'I don't wish to do so. You're my wife. But there's no alternative. Mzee Matata is crafty and cunning. He may well say that he accepts my sacrifice and that the gods are appeased and still secretly plan my death. I'm no longer safe here.'

'It's a big thing you ask of me,' said Seitu. 'But you're my husband.' She paused and then added firmly, 'Yes, Ngurumo, I'll go with you. I'll go anywhere with you.'

Joy lept into Ngurumo's heart. 'You won't be sorry,' he said and he embraced her.

But there were shadows in Seitu's eyes which seemed to indicate that she was by no means definitely sure.

4   Having decided that they would move, Ngurumo and Seitu began to prepare secretly.

'Let's make sure Mzee Matata doesn't know we are leaving,' Ngurumo whispered, 'otherwise he'll prevent us from going.'

'But how shall we move our things without being found out?' Seitu replied.

'I shall go to the new land under cover of darkness

taking with me some of our belongings. Then, without telling anyone, we shall set out finally with anything remaining and our goats.'

'But how do we get food to eat before we harvest what we have planted?'

'There are plenty of bananas and wild tubers and fruits. The stretch of the river over there is teeming with fish. Occasionally, I shall hunt for game.'

'It'll be dangerous going through the forest at night.'

'I shall be all right. I have spear and I don't think there will be any difficulty.'

'Until you return safely, my anxiety will be great.'

'Have no fears,' he said.

He did not dare make the journey until he was quite sure that everyone in the village was asleep. Even then he moved with extreme caution. He clung to the shadows until the last of the huts was behind him. He tried to double his speed but was encumbered with belongings – a hoe, a crudely shaped axe, a short, broad sword for weeding and some household effects. In his right hand, at the ready, he carried his spear.

The journey through the forest taxed his nerves to the utmost. His way was lit only by the faint moonlight that filtered through the trees. He grew increasingly tense. All round him were rustlings and hissings. These sounds, he knew, were made by nothing more danger-ous than leaves and grass stirring in the wind. But in the inky darkness, they took on a sinister tone. At one place, he heard what sounded like the patter and padding of feet. At another a grunting was not far away. The chatterings and growlings added to his tension. Once he paused and turned, his eyes combing the darkness behind him, his spear raised, convinced that an animal was stalking him. After some moments he was able to relax. He kept on casting nervous glances over his shoulder as he went along.

Suddenly, there was a scream almost at his very feet. As it died in a gurgle, he realised that a night bird had claimed a rodent. The shock had set his heart racing and sweat poured down his body. Once, a bird or a bat brushed against his face, causing him to catch his breath in alarm. At last, he was clear of the forest belt. He could see now the vast sky alive with a myriad of stars and above him was the thin sliver of the moon. The air came sweet and clean to his nostrils. He inhaled deeply, the tension gradually seeping out of him. The night wind was cool and soothing. He could see the tall, closely-growing grass in dark silhouette and the great shadow of the mountains standing like vast sentinels above the valley.

Eventually, he came to the end of the journey. Here, he thought, he and Seitu would find peace and contentment. There would be ample food for their needs. At first they would feel lonely but he was sure others would join them later. In any case, he was one who enjoyed a quiet life.

Having left the articles he had brought where he would readily find them again, he took another look at the land. He did not know that the range of mountains he so much admired was one of the main obstacles that had prevented his tribe being discovered. They cut off the approach from the other side where people were living a much more sophisticated life than the inhabitants of Pachanga could imagine possible. Beyond the mountains lived Africans and white men together.

The people of Pachanga had always lived within the enclaves of the triangular mountain ranges. They had seen the mountains surrounding them as an impenetrable barrier. They did not know that some fifty miles beyond was a territory that stretched hundreds of miles and took in many villages and towns. All the people inhabiting the island belonged to the same race and spoke one language with its various dialects. But to the people of Pachanga, the world literally ended at the horizon within the confines of the mountains. They lived in their own enclosed, isolated world, observing customs and usages, methods of farming and social arrangements which were outmoded.

Standing there in the bright moon-lit night, Ngurumo felt that the Land of the East was a great land – a land that flowed with richness and vitality. People would grow strong on it and regain the confidence and joy he knew his people had lost.

He returned home without anything happening to cause him alarm and while there was still darkness to cover his movements.

'Ahhhh!' It was a great sigh of relief with which he was greeted by Seitu. In the darkness he felt his way towards her. Seitu's hand found his arm and drew him down to her side.

'Everything is all right,' he told her.

'No one has seen you?'

'I don't think so.'

'Oh, I'm so glad. I've been greatly worried.'

'That wasn't necessary.' He touched her. He found that she was trembling. He began to stroke her reassuringly.

'I'm sure more than ever that we're doing the right

thing,' he said. 'We can lead a marvellous life there.'

Her body became still. He sensed that she felt calm and secure in his embrace, her mouth was warm and moist against his throat. Delight leapt in him. She whimpered with a joy that was beyond expectation. He was lost in a world of incredible sensation.

The next day, however, reaction set in. Seitu, never as confident as he was about the move to the Land of the East, was in a subdued state of mind. Ngurumo was aware that the mind of the female was often unstable. He had known his mother and his sisters waver after making important decisions. Seitu, much as he loved her, had her full measure of this womanly weakness. Having made up her mind once, she began to question the wisdom of what she had decided.

'Listen,' he pleaded, 'we're doing what we have to do. Let's do it with a good heart.'

Although she said nothing her demeanour indicated that he had not fully convinced her and that her heart was dark with doubts. However, she became firm and positive in her decision a few days later following an incident which nearly cost Ngurumo his life.

Mzee Matata ordered some of the young men, together with three or four elders, to go out hunting. There was an urgent need for meat and the purpose was to secure gazelle and, if possible, buffalo. A party of about twenty, Ngurumo amongst them, set out early one morning to hunt. They were armed with bows and poisoned arrows and spears. Poison was obtained from shrubs, barks or roots. It was made in varying strengths; some could rapidly kill its victim. Several effective antidotes were also available.

Their leader, appointed by Mzee Matata, was Abedi,

44

known to be a cunning and able hunter. All of them were wearing amulets and their favourite mascots to bring luck and avert catastrophe. They made their way to where water was likely to draw game. The first pools they came to were not deserted. At one of them lions were drinking and near another a pair of tigers were sleeping. No smaller game would venture near when such swift and powerful enemies were around. It was necessary to go deeper into the jungle.

The motionless air became oven hot as the day advanced. The trek through the forest over little-used tracks began to sap their energies. The rough, uneven ground had effect on the leg muscles. Many a time, they had to climb over the fallen trunks of trees. But no one suggested there should be a pause for rest. The need to secure meat was well understood by all concerned and they did not wish to be in the deep and dark recess of the jungle after night had fallen.

Moving along in the place alloted to him, Ngurumo looked at Abedi. He was a squat man noted for his unwillingness to talk. He rarely said anything, being content to make himself understood by gestures of direction and command. It was known that he enjoyed the favours of Mzee Matata and the people treated him with a nervous respect. He had the ears of the man who could intercede with the gods to bring harm on anyone the fetish priest or Abedi himself did not like.

The day was at its hottest when they came upon a water-hole beside which two gazelles were grazing. One was a fine buck with proud antlers and the other, smaller and more slender, was a doe. The hunters halted when the animals were still out of range as the

45

least hint of danger would send them racing and leaping away, not to be seen again.

Abedi beckoned to Ngurumo to join him. Ngurumo moved silently forward. He guessed that Abedi intended to make use of his known skill as a hunter. He inched forward with great caution. Reaching him, Abedi asked him to go ahead and when within range, to take aim at the buck. Ngurumo nodded in agreement and moved on. He scanned the ground carefully before taking each step to avoid treading on any twig that might snap and so alert the animals of his presence.

Abedi crept behind him, ostensibly to fling his spear at the doe when the right moment came. Ngurumo continued steadily to close the gap between himself and the buck. He admired the graceful look of the game. It moved with a supple ease and a hint of vibrancy that suggested a rare alertness. Occasionally, it paused in its grazing to raise its slender, delicate head and sniff the air. Reassured, the head went down to the grass again.

Ngurumo was now within range. He finally halted and drew back his right arm, posing his spear in line with the forehead of the buck. If his aim was correct, the animal would die within seconds of the spear's poisoned barb entering the flesh.

Ngurumo launched his spear. At the same moment there was a shout of warning from behind him. Instinctively, he flung himself to the ground. As his body made contact with the ground, there was a thud somewhere above his head. He glanced up. Quivering in the trunk of the tree directly in front of him was a spear. It needed no calculation for him to realize that, had he remained upright, the spear would have pierced

46

his body in the region of the heart, certainly killing him instantly as his own spear had slain the buck. The doe had vanished.

Slowly Ngurumo got up on his feet and looked behind him. Abedi was hurrying towards him.

'A mistake,' he was saying breathlessly, as he reached him. 'Are you all right?'

Ngurumo looked again at the place where he was standing and at the spot where the doe had been grazing. He had by no means been in line with the animal.

'A mistake?' Ngurumo queried. 'What sort of mistake?'

'My hand lost its hold on the spear as I was aiming at the doe.'

'Then who shouted?' Ngurumo was bristling with suspicion. Abedi could not meet his gaze and there was something furtive in his manner.

'I asked you, who shouted?' Ngurumo said hotly. 'It wasn't your voice I heard.'

The rest of the hunters had drawn near looking at them enquiringly. It was Bakari who broke the silence. He had been Ngurumo's friend from their childhood days.

'I shouted,' he said.

'Why did you shout?' Ngurumo asked.

Bakari did not answer. Ngurumo knew why. There was no need for Bakari to say anything more. Abedi's demeanour was not that of a man who was sorry for his action.

'You deliberately threw your spear at me.' Ngurumo accused him and then he seized Abedi by the shoulders.

'N–n–no——no!'

'You meant to kill me.'

'N–n–no!'

'Why no? That was why you sent me ahead of you the way you did.' Ngurumo began to shake Abedi violently. 'Why did you wish to kill me?' he demanded. 'When did I do you any harm?'

'Never, never!'

'Then why did you try to murder me?'

'I didn't. I wish you no harm.'

'So you were acting upon instructions.' Ngurumo shook Abedi so savagely it seemed that the man's head would be loosened from its neck.

'Who instructed you to kill me? Speak out! Do you hear? Speak out!'

Abedi's eyes were bulging in alarm and his teeth were rattling in his mouth. He was pale with fear but he did not intend to speak. Ngurumo flung him away with an impatient gesture. Abedi went sprawling heavily on his back.

'We had better get the buck ready to carry it back to the village,' Ngurumo said. He felt heavy at heart. He knew quite well, as did all the rest, who had given Abedi directives to kill him. The hunt had been arranged for the purpose of having him murdered.

The sight of the buck, still and wide-eyed in death, served to increase Ngurumo's depression. The animal had been so beautiful, so charged with life; and now it lay, its skull shattered, its long face blood-stained, its limbs stiffening. It would provide the people of Pachanga with much-needed meat.

He watched in silence as a branch was stripped and the legs of the buck were tied together. The pole was pushed between the animal's legs and, upside down, it was lifted from the ground. With Abedi in the lead, they

48

began the long trek back to the village. There was no need for silence but no one talked. They had witnessed an attempt at murder and the fact subdued them.

Ngurumo brought up the rear of the column. Should he tell Seitu that Abedi, acting on Mzee Matata's orders, had attempted to kill him? The news would cause her alarm. He realized that he must tell her. If he did not, someone else would and she might well attribute his refusal to break the news to her to the wrong motives.

Back home at last, his expression revealed to Seitu that something was amiss. Her anxiety was such that she was on the alert for unusual news.

'You caught nothing?' she asked.

'We managed to kill a very fine buck. There'll be meat for everyone for at least one meal.'

'Then why do you look so despondent?'

'Because Abedi tried to kill me.'

The breath went out of her with a shocked hiss.

'Obviously on Mzee Matata's orders,' Ngurumo added. He went on to narrate all that had happened during the hunting expedition.

'He'll try again,' Seitu said. 'What are we to do?'

'I've already decided. We must make our final preparations and leave as soon as possible. Of course if you would prefer to stay. . . .'

'No, no! I would rather die with you.'

This statement by Seitu overwhelmed him. He drew her nearer and kissed her on the forehead.

'Let's think, not of dying, but of living together,' he said. 'We're still young and the future belongs to us.'

He spoke with a confidence he was far from feeling. He was sure that Mzee Matata would not relax his efforts to bring about his death. The fact that the

49

abortive attempt had been seen by so many witnesses would force the fetish priest to accomplish his purpose as soon as possible.

Mzee Matata claimed that the gods conferred on him unlimited powers. It would not do for the people to see that Ngurumo was immune from those powers. That would cause the people to ask questions and begin to doubt whether their fetish priest was really as powerful as he claimed to be. There was no doubt that Mzee Matata would strike again and that there would be no room for error in his second attempt.

During the next few days, Ngurumo visited the Land of the East every night; not always to take personal effects there, for his belongings were few, but to build enclosures in which to keep his domestic animals. He also worked on a house for Seitu and himself. He had given a great deal of thought to the kind of house he was building. It was round but spacious. The materials were reeds tied together with the stem of the creeping plant and then plastered with mud. The roof would be thatched with shingles to last longer than the fronds of the palm tree or grass. When completed, he would decorate the outside walls with mouldings of a lion in pursuit of a gazelle it would never catch. For some reason this idea appealed to him.

Ngurumo intended to make a doorway that would be high enough to admit even the tallest man without his having to stoop.

There were also to be apertures in the walls that would let in plenty of light and air. All the huts in Pachanga tended to be gloomy inside because they had either only very small windows or no windows at all. This was because people were in their rooms only when it was dark or when they were sleeping. Most of the day was spent in the fields working or outside under the shades of trees talking or playing games; sometimes people drank palm wine tapped from the palm tree.

The nights he spent away from his hut preparing for removal to the new home were nights of strain. There was always the danger of an encounter with wild beasts and he could not be sure that he had succeeded in keeping his movements secret from the village and that he would not be attacked either on his way there or back.

As the days passed and nothing untoward happened, his confidence increased. The gods, if they disapproved of what he was doing, had shown no sign of it. Everything seemed to be going well. At last, everything needed at the new home had been taken there except for their two goats. These, Ngurumo had decided, might betray them. Their bleats in the night were certain to arouse the village. But he could not go without them. They were the basis of his future prosperity. He therefore decided on a plan. There was a herb which grew in the forest and which had remarkable power to induce sleep. A man had only to boil the leaves and drink some of the water in which they had been cooked and immediately he would be put into a deep sleep for a long period. Ngurumo fetched some of the leaves. He would mix them with the goats' evening meal before he and Seitu made their move. If the herb affected animals as it did men, then the goats would be asleep while they were being carried to the new home.

On their last day in the village, both felt a growing sense of agitation. They were making an irretrievable break with the past and they would not be allowed to return to the place where they had been born and had spent all their days. There were strong ties neither wished to break but there was no other alternative.

The sun at last dipped towards the horizon. Ngurumo was standing at the entrance of his hut when the sun went down and the stars took over in what appeared to be a vast jumble of glittering points of brightness. He went into the hut.

'How are you feeling?' he asked his wife.

'Sad and rather frightened.'

'I don't think there is anything to worry about. Once we're settled in our new home, we shall be really happy. This I can assure you.'

'If only others were going to live there with us,' she said.

'They'll join us there especially when there's nothing to eat and they're hungry. We shall soon prove to be the saviours of our people.'

'How can we do that?'

'When the people see that they're faced with starvation, they'll come to us and we shall be in a position to help them. You see, the land there is so fertile, I intend to cultivate more than we ourselves shall need. I mean to cultivate such a large piece that we can feed many people. It won't be hard work. The land is so rich it'll produce a lot for very little effort.'

Seitu did not share her husband's optimism. She continued to harbour the feeling that Mzee Matata would not allow them to escape without doing his utmost to destroy them. That he had not acted against them since Abedi tried to kill Ngurumo during the last hunt did not reassure her. She knew the fetish priest had held his hand only because he meant to succeed when he struck again. There had been many witnesses of that first abortive attempt and prestige required that he succeed in destroying Ngurumo (and perhaps his wife) so that the people would continue to have confidence in him and the gods.

Seitu had said all she had to say. Ngurumo was her man and there was nothing she could do but follow him wherever he went. He had been chosen for her by the gods and they knew that he was the right man for her. Deep in her own heart she knew he was the right husband too.

There was something she had not yet mentioned to her husband. It was something she had decided she would tell him only after they had settled in their new home. It was something she felt sure would delight him. Within her, marvellously and most mysteriously, had sprung into existence a new life. It thrilled her to realize it. She knew it was their love for each other which had resulted in this miracle of a new life.

5   Ngurumo found the journey to the new home the most testing he had made. He fed the goats with the herb and they fell into a state of unconsciousness. But he was worried in case he had given them too much of the sleep-inducing leaves and had killed them, for they showed no sign of life; they lay as if they were dead.

He decided he would carry one and Seitu the other. He also carried the remaining items they had left in their hut until they were ready to move, a few cooking and drinking pots for their daily use. His right hand would carry only one thing, his spear, ready for instant action.

Knowing his wife would be very nervous, he gave her another spear in the hope that it would give her a little confidence.

'I shall go ahead,' he told her, 'and you must keep close behind me. The forest seems a bit more frightening at night than during daylight but I'm sure we shall be all right.'

They sat in silence in their hut for what seemed to them a long time. It was night but the mere presence of darkness was not enough. They waited until the stillness had deepened so that every sound could be easily identified. Everything they were to take with them had been made ready. At last, Ngurumo whispered, 'Come, my wife,' and they lifted up their remaining belongings.

Ngurumo stood at the door of the hut for a few moments before he stepped into the open. Then he halted again, listening. Satisfied that it was safe to proceed, he beckoned to Seitu. They walked cautiously between the huts, making for the forest.

The night was cool. There was more wind than usual and the branches rustled and creaked. Ngurumo felt tense. Should they be overheard or seen, an alarm would be raised. There was a bad moment when, from inside a hut they were passing, there was a sudden shout. They froze. Ngurumo had a prickly feeling. But no one appeared. Later, he realized the noise was probably made by someone having a nightmare.

There was no moonlight. The wind kept the trees and bushes in a state of agitation. There were crackings and the inevitable night noises of growlings and howlings. At some places the path was overgrown with dense bushes and they had to move step by step, pausing every now and then to explore the ground immediately in front of them lest they step on a snake lying across the path.

Ngurumo had a special fear. There was the danger that a lion or a tiger might scent the kids they were carrying. If that happened, he knew they would be attacked.

At one moment a savage snarling broke out only a few steps from them. Seitu screamed. Ngurumo dropped his load, and clasped her hand.

'Animals fighting,' he said. 'Come. They won't trouble us while they're so engaged with one another.'

But Seitu was unable to move a step. Shock had so robbed her legs of strength that she could not walk. They were still at the same spot when the sounds of fighting reached a crescendo and then gradually died out in a gurgle. Then there remained only the wind-fanned noises.

'Now,' Ngurumo patted Seitu on the back, 'let's move on.'

He picked up his load and helped Seitu to carry hers. Seitu was in such a state she found herself calling on the gods to protect them.

Incident followed incident. Reaching a clearing, they heard a loud squealing and the thudding of hoofs. For one heart-stopping moment Ngurumo feared a beast was rushing on them. He was not taking chances, and with spear raised, he was ready to strike. But it swerved away a short distance from him, evidently on flight along a customary escape route.

'Nothing but a wild boar,' he said, disgusted with himself for not realising at once what kind of animal they had disturbed. Nonetheless, the heat of fear churned in his stomach. As for Seitu, she was weeping openly, her hands over her face and trembling as she endeavoured to resist the hysteria that threatened to take hold of her.

'It's all right,' he told her, 'we're quite safe.'

It was not easy for Seitu to regain her self-control and it was some time before they could continue the journey.

'We have only a little way to go,' he said. 'Soon – very soon – we shall be safely in our new home.'

They had, in fact a longer way to go than he said, and when they reached the edge of the jungle, he paused and put down his load, his heart pounding very fast. Seitu did likewise, her heart also breathing restlessly. They sat on the turfy ground for a short rest.

'The worst is over,' he told her.

When they were more composed, they resumed the journey. It had been a slow journey and the first light of a new day was beginning to press darkness from the eastern sky when they finally reached the vast plains where Ngurumo had erected their new home.

'Now there's nothing more to fear,' he assured her. 'We are quite, quite safe.'

Seitu was so relieved she began to laugh a little. Ngurumo realised what an ordeal the journey had been for her. He knew well that she was terrified even before they set off, but for his sake, she had undertaken the journey. He felt great pride in her. Not many girls would have been so loyal and trusting.

'I built the house beside the stream that crosses the plains,' he explained. 'We have water only a little way from our door. There are many fish in it.'

By the time they reached their destination, daylight had taken over from the darkness of the night. While still some distance away, he paused and smiled at her expectantly.

'You will like your new home. It's ready for us to live in.'

Seitu was surprised at what she saw. The house was bigger than any she had seen before except that in which Mzee Matata lived.

'We need a big house for the family that may soon come,' Ngurumo added, noting her delight.

Seitu laughed. She bent her head and gazed at the goats lying helplessly on the ground and asked, 'Do you think they are dead?'

Ngurumo was afraid that they were, but did not say so.

'We'll put them in the enclosure I've made at the back of the house. That's all we can do now, Seitu.'

After the long and tiring journey with its unexpected hazards, they were, unusually hungry. Their first meal at the new home was a rich breakfast of wild fruits and bananas. They ate like hungry wolves and then lay down on the mats for a rest and soon they were asleep. They slept for most of the day; the fatigue of the walk wore off.

When Ngurumo awoke, it was to the sound of bleating. At first the significance of it failed to strike him. Then he realized what it meant. He shook his wife gently.

'Seitu, Seitu, wake up! The goats are alive. I can hear them bleating.'

Seitu blinked her eyes half open and looked around blankly.

'Goats?' she mumbled. 'What goats?'

'Those we brought with us.'

She understood then and was awake at once. She raised her shapely arms and stretched them. Then she stretched her legs. Ngurumo stood up.

'There's much to be done,' he said. 'But first, we must wash. Come on.'

Holding her hand, he led Seitu out into the open. It was already past mid-day and the air was filled with heat.

'Look!' he said, indicating the surroundings with a sweep of his arm. 'This is where we're to live. Isn't it worth all the trouble we had during the journey in the dark?'

Seitu made a quick turn around. Eastward to the foot of the mighty thrust of mountains, the land looked like a vast green sea. Westward was the curving line of the edge of the jungle. Only a stone's throw away, the gurgling water of the stream sparkled in the bright sunlight.

'It flows into the Kankan,' Ngurumo said with authority, 'and it will provide us with fish as well as the water we shall need.'

Hand in hand, they walked slowly towards it.

'There's a pool over there, deep enough for us to swim in. We'll come here first thing every morning and wash the sleep out of our eyes and put the cool-ness of the water on our bodies.'

They discarded all but their loin-cloths and waded

into the stream. Soon they were both swimming. Ever since they could remember, they had always played in the Kankan river. Like most of the people of Pachanga, they were skilful swimmers. Ngurumo could stay under water for a surprising length of time, resurfacing far away from where he had dived.

There had always been the danger of crocodiles. No one felt quite safe when washing or swimming in the river. Children had sometimes been snatched into the jaws of the monsters and had been carried away screaming and struggling in vain. Here, however, there was no danger of crocodiles. The stream was narrow but they could wash and disport themselves without fear or care. Ngurumo lay on his back, floating on the water. He watched Seitu as she waded out to the bank. There seemed to be a physical change in her he had not noticed before. She had the air of one who had achieved a vital aim.

Wondering what it might be, he eyed her carefully. He was sure her legs and arms were the same. Her breasts and stomach were rather fuller, standing out more prominently than before. Her expression intrigued him. Despite the ordeal of the previous night and the strangeness and newness of the surroundings, she looked contented. He was at a loss to understand the reason.

She stood on the bank, gracefully at ease, allowing the sun to dry her. He swam towards her. He was struck by the loveliness of her form. Looking up at her, he saw her silhouette against the sky as if she had been standing on a pedestal. He felt stirrings of delight. He advanced until he was standing right in front of her. Drops of water still gleamed on her body.

'There's much to do,' Ngurumo told her. 'While you make a meal, I'll go and look after the goats. By the sound they're making, they are hungry.'

The animals had taken no food because of their drugged sleep. Now they were very active, foraging for food. Ngurumo uprooted some tubers, peeled off the skin, diced them and left them in the pen. He returned to Seitu.

'I've already cleared a large tract of land and I've planted maize on it. Before harvest time our chickens will have hatched new ones and the goats will have multiplied.'

'That's splendid, my husband.'

He had other plans too, he told Seitu. He wanted to widen the narrow part of the stream into a large swimming pool. He intended to plant bouganvillaea in front of the house as a decoration. Using branches of trees and vines, he was going to build enclosures for the chickens and with thorn bushes he would build a fence around the house to protect themselves from attacks by wild animals.

'Here there's beauty, but we must also have safety and that's something we ourselves must provide.'

'It seems we shall be working very hard for some time.'

'Yes, but we shall gain great reward for our labour. In Pachanga we also worked hard and there was nothing showing for all that we did. Here, we shall have well-bred animals and abundance of crops. Besides, we shall find life more pleasant as time goes on. We shall get more and more for less labour. That's the way things work out when there's good soil.'

In the days that followed, both worked really hard.

They were so eager to translate their dreams into reality that they worked in the fields even when the day was at its hottest. They wanted to make quick progress. Until they could produce their own food, they lived mostly on fruits and tubers, and variety was provided by an occasional chicken or game. This formed healthier diet than they were used to in Pachanga.

One night, as they were sitting in the bright moonlight in front of their house resting after the day's labour and enjoying the cool breeze, Seitu revealed the secret of her happiness.

'My husband,' she said, 'I'm heavy with child.'

He looked at her with that appreciation she had grown to expect and there welled up in him a great tenderness for her.

'Oh, my dear!' he exclaimed. He embraced her. He did not know what to say but he felt emotions he had never experienced before.

'That's good news,' he said, beaming.

Then he withdrew from her.

'I've noticed a change in you but I couldn't understand what it was about. So we're going to have a child.' A loud uncontrolled laugh gushed out in sheer delight. 'I told you this was a fruitful land.'

She too laughed. She was pleased by his reaction.

'This is the natural outcome of marriage,' she said teasingly.

'Yes, but it's still marvellous beyond words.'

She nodded.

'Now, we really must make a success of our new land and home,' he told her. 'We shall be building, not only for ourselves, but also for those who may come after us.'

C

'Yes,' she agreed.

'You know,' Ngurumo went on, 'I think we should plan the new village that will spring up here. In Pachanga, the huts were built close together and just anywhere. It'll be better if over here the houses aren't so near to one another. They'll have much more light and air. And I have also thought of something else.'

'My husband, you're always thinking of something new,' Seitu cut in. 'What is it this time?'

'I know of a way to get rid of the refuse. We should not just throw it away.'

Seitu stared at him in astonishment mingled with wonder.

'What more can we do?' she asked disparagingly.

'Haven't you noticed how flies and other insects gathered in such large numbers on refuse in Pachanga? They buzz about and sometimes bite, which hurts. They torment babies and little children.'

'It's true.'

'It seems to me that if we have no refuse, flies and other insects won't be around.' He waved a hand to indicate the new land. 'There are no flies here. Only some tiny insects, but they seem to be food for the birds and they won't cause us any harm. Why then are there large numbers of flies at Pachanga and none here? Don't you think it's because we haven't any refuse here to attract them?'

Seitu listened attentively as Ngurumo continued to propound his theory.

'We can carry the refuse far from our house. That's one way. But I think there's yet another. I can dig a channel from the stream down to the river; divert water into it and the refuse will be washed away.'

She eyed him with admiration.

'Always you're thinking of something new. I don't know whether your channel idea can work but there's no harm in trying it. Before then, we can carry the refuse a long way from the house to keep the flies away.'

'That's what we'll do first. The channel can't be made now, for there are more urgent things to do. One day I'll construct it and see to it that it does what we want it to do.'

They were silent. Then Seitu still full of doubts about their escape asked Ngurumo, 'D'you think the gods are pleased that we've come here?'

'I'm sure they are. Why should they make a land so good and so friendly if they don't want us to make use of it?'

'That I don't know,' she said. 'But Mzee Matata said that the gods would be angry if we moved.'

'Have they been angry? And what are the signs? Haven't we done well here since we came, even though our first days are bound to be difficult?'

'Yes, we've done very well.'

'We shall do even better. The days ahead will be full of joy and improvement. We have nothing to fear.'

But he was unaware of what was happening back in Pachanga, where Mzee Matata was plotting against them.

6   In Pachanga, the disappearance of Ngurumo and Seitu had created a great sensation. No one could remember anyone vanishing in such a manner before. In all the oral tradition

and history of the people there had been no mention of anyone deserting the tribe.

Naturally, everyone turned to Mzee Matata for an explanation. He was at first greatly tempted to tell them that the missing couple had been spirited away by the gods as a punishment for Ngurumo daring to question the wisdom of their fetish priest, Mzee Matata himself. But the fact that the pair had taken all their belongings with them made such an explanation unlikely. Prudently he offered no such excuse for their absence. Besides they might return and their presence would then make him look very awkward. Mzee Matata had good reason for appearing to be far-seeing.

Although he had not said so, not even to Fundi, his closest confidant, Ngurumo's escape both enraged and disturbed him; it had also undermined confidence in him. He was determined to regain his waning popularity at the first opportunity.

'Fundi,' he called his henchman, 'is there dissatisfaction among the people?'

'They're worried,' Fundi replied guardedly. 'The declining harvests are causing them concern. Some people are beginning to feel the pangs of hunger. That doesn't make them as contented as they used to be.'

It was the reply Mzee Matata had expected.

'No one can question the actions of the gods,' he said. 'If the people suffer hunger it's because they've displeased the gods. The flight of Ngurumo and Seitu shows that there's disobedience.'

'D'you know where they've gone to?'

'I shall consult the gods. They'll reveal to me where they are.'

In fact, Mzee Matata knew where they were. It was

64

obvious after speaking of the fertile Land of the East that that was where the pair had gone. But he pretended that he owed his knowledge, as well as his power, to the gods. He had to make a show of consulting them.

'What d'you want to do?' Fundi asked.

'That I haven't yet decided. At the moment, there's nothing we need to do – except one thing.'

'And that is what?'

'We'll have to make sure that Ngurumo and his wife are where the gods say. I'll consult them immediately. Then we'll send Abedi to see exactly where they are. The gods often give only very general directions.'

If ever Mzee Matata's prophesies went wrong or the gods did not act as expected, he tried to justify them. When this happened, he blamed not the gods, but the people.

He took out his sacred cowries and laid them in their correct magical order on the sand in front of him. He weaved his hands over them, his eyes half closed as if he was in a trance. He muttered the time-honoured incantations. He lifted up first one cowrie and then another, arranging them to form squares, triangles and circles. Eventually, having arranged the cowries – ostensibly to the satisfaction of the gods – he pointed to the east.

'There,' he announced, 'there, beyond the wedge of the jungle to the east, Ngurumo and his wife will be found.'

He opened his eyes and nodded confidently.

'That's where the gods say they are.'

'D'you wish Abedi to go there and see?' Fundi enquired.

'Yes. But he mustn't be seen by them. Tell him that. No matter what, he mustn't be seen.'

Fundi bowed indicating understanding and respect. Then he went in search of Abedi. He rejoined Mzee Matata minutes later.

'Abedi is to make the journey tonight,' Fundi told him. 'He'll use the cloak of darkness.'

'That's good,' the fetish priest agreed.

The next day, Abedi was able to report that he had seen where Ngurumo and Seitu were living.

'The gods command that you say not a word about this to anyone,' Mzee Matata warned him. 'Whisper so much as a syllable even to your wife about what you've seen and you'll surely die.'

Abedi looked perturbed.

'The gods have sealed my lips,' he said.

Mzee Matata was, in fact, playing a very cunning game. The people, he knew, were becoming more and more worried over the deteriorating food situation. The flight of Ngurumo and Seitu had upset them. Mzee Matata had in the renegades just what he needed to demonstrate the power of the gods and to ensure his own position of absolute authority.

The days went by, adding themselves up to the coming and going of no less than twelve moons. Another two harvests were reaped but very little was gathered. The people were beginning to face the most serious crisis of their existence. The shortage of food, now chronic, meant that they were suffering from real hunger. The men had turned to daily hunting in order to supplement the scanty diet. They fished further up and down the river than before. While these activities helped to ease the ache of hunger to some extent, they were by no means the permanent solution. Through Fundi and Abedi, and other informers, Mzee Matata knew full well the mood of the people. As their hunger increased, so did their concern and dissatisfaction.

'It's time to act,' the fetish priest decided.

He called Fundi to his palace. He spoke to him softly and urgently. Fundi felt the plot was a good one. Provided all went well, it was bound to prove the power of the gods.

Dusk was gathering and the people were grouped here and there talking together before dispersing to their huts to sleep. This was how they had behaved for moons past. They talked over the events of the day; they gossiped. They discussed those who were expecting babies, those who were sick and those who were near to dying.

Suddenly, in a tree on the fringe of the village appeared a ball of flame. It rose into the air and fell, spluttering on to one of the huts. A cry of consternation and alarm went up from the people. Within seconds the roof of the hut had caught fire. Flames were rapidly devouring it. For some time there was confusion. The initial terror kept the people immobile. Then there was a rush to get water. While efforts were being made to put out the fire, the occupants were dashing in and out of the hut rescuing their belongings. The hut was completely destroyed but no damage was done to anyone nearby. Having quenched the fire, the people remained outside talking nervously in the darkness. Fearing there might be more fireballs, they looked skyward. They were sure the fire was some sort of a sign from the gods. That was how they spoke when they were particularly angry. They hurled fire from the sky.

In the darkness and confusion, no one had seen Fundi in the tree. Nor did anyone see him climb down and slip away. He appeared amongst them.

'Mzee Matata has a message for you,' he said. 'You're all to gather at the sacred ground in front of his house in the morning. The gods have a special message for you. They've also told Mzee Matata that there'll be no more fireballs thrown on you tonight. You may go to your homes in peace and enjoy your sleep.'

There was a murmur of relief. The people dispersed to their huts.

The next morning after breakfast, they gathered in an arc before the house of the fetish priest. They knew they would have to wait for some time. Mzee Matata would not appear until there had been time to build up a sense of expectancy. At last, preceded by Abedi, Mzee Matata appeared. He advanced to his usual position before the stone of sacrifice. He raised his arm and glanced about commandingly.

'The gods are very angry with you,' he began. 'You've bred renegades. This the gods won't tolerate. They've been patiently waiting for many moons for the deserters to return. This they haven't done. The patience of the gods is exhausted. Last night, they hurled a fireball upon our village. That consumed only one hut. They warn me that, unless the renegades are punished, they will send more fireballs that will destroy all the buildings and all your belongings. They are bent on destroying you utterly.'

There was a murmur of dismay.

'The gods demand that those who have deserted the land of their forefathers be brought back and sacrificed. That's the only offering that will appease them before

68

they bestow favour on you. Your crops will then grow fat. You'll have abundance of food. There'll be a new era of prosperity for all of you.'

'Ahhhh!' They cried out in great relief. If only these promises would come true.

'The sacrifice,' Mzee Matata explained, 'will be made like that of all living creatures.'

'Ooooooohhhhhh!' This time there was a note of repudiation in the sound. All knew what the fetish priest meant.

'I shall detail twelve men to go and bring back Ngurumo and his wife,' Mzee Matata told them. 'They'll go at once. Tomorrow, the renegades will be offered to the gods as they demand.'

He began to single out the men. Having finished, he instructed them to take their spears, bows and arrows and set out under the command of Fundi.

*   *   *

At their new home, Ngurumo and Seitu were well pleased with the life they were leading. The moons which had come and gone since their arrival had been well used. They had created a home that was far superior to anything anyone in Pachanga had known. The new house was roomy. It had a window and a door-way. These allowed the circulation of air. A reed mat made by Seitu screened the entrance. Inside, there were stools and a table, as well as sleeping mats. Ngurumo had made the furniture and although it was crude, having been constructed of roughly shaped logs, it was strong and served their purpose well.

In front of the house were several acres of cleared land and on them was growing the second crop of maize. Like the first, it promised to be abundant. Behind the house Ngurumo had planted varieties of fruits and these were flourishing. There were now four goats and all were doing well. The chickens had increased in number. There was a daily supply of eggs. In fact, they were living, they felt, royally.

Ngurumo had built enclosures for the livestock. He was in the process of building a fence of thorn bushes that would protect their house from wild beasts. There had been some frightening times in the past. The rich grass drew animals such as deer, zebra, and rodents to graze on it. They in turn attracted ferocious animals like lion and the tiger and these had of course noticed the presence of goats and chickens. There had been one particular night when Ngurumo had been awakened to hear sniffing and growling. Knowing that a lion was prowling close to the house, he picked up his spear and moved to the doorway. In the moonlight he saw the animal in front of their home. He stood still watching it moving. It sniffed about enquiringly. Then, to his dismay, it began to move towards him.

He shouted and waved his spear. The lion snarled but it did not retreat.

'Away with you!' Ngurumo shouted again, banging his spear on the ground. He could hear a cry behind him. He had awakened the baby. This meant Seitu was awake too and probably holding the baby in fear.

'Go away!' Ngurumo yelled, advancing a step forward towards the lion. There was a defiant growl and a twitching of the tail. Ngurumo was sweating profusely. His teeth were chattering. The hand gripping the spear was shaking. He wanted to run away. But if he did, the lion would spring upon him and tear him into pieces.

'Be gone!' Ngurumo had never shouted so loudly in his life. At the same time he waved the spear wildly to frighten the animal; but it responded with a snarl. Then it began to retreat. At first, it did so one slow step backward at a time as if still pondering over what to do next. Then it turned and padded away.

Ngurumo leaned against the wall taking into his lungs desperately needed air. The tension was over but his heart was still beating very fast. Regaining his strength, he returned to the house.

'Everything is all right,' he told Seitu.

He lay down, his arm stretched on her torso while she soothed the baby.

The birth of the baby had been the most wonderful experience of his whole life. He had acted as midwife. All the girls of Pachanga were taught about midwifery, so Seitu had been able to tell him what to do. Birth came easily. The child served to draw Ngurumo and Seitu more closely together. Both marvelled that their love had resulted in a chubby, dark eyed infant. They would admire the beauty of the face, the crinkly black hair, the big wondering eyes and equally, the smoothness of the skin and the tiny perfectly formed fingers.

There was such a deep feeling for Seitu on the part of Ngurumo that it required no physical expression. He was deeply content simply to sit with her and admire her. Her breasts were still large but her stomach had returned to its former slim shape. She was as lithe and graceful as before.

Ngurumo had carried out his plan of diverting part of the stream to carry away the refuse. It had not been altogether successful but it had worked in part. He was proved right about the flies. They were not troubled by

71

the great swarms which had made life such a torment in the village of their birth.

Because food grew so readily and in such abundance, after the first few moons, they had more leisure than they had known when they were living in Pachanga. There were days when they could sit out together in the afternoon just resting or playing with the child. These were golden days filled with a deep peace and contentment. It was on one of these occasions that Seitu looked at him in a way that was different. She was smiling but more to herself than at him and her lips were slightly parted. She was breathing rather quickly. Her breasts were rising and falling rapidly.

'My husband,' she said, 'do you love me?'

He smiled back.

'You know that I love you,' he said.

She was delighted. She moved to him so that she could readily touch him. Her hand came to rest on his shoulder. Then it moved to the chest. It was deeply muscled and she liked to touch it for the same reason that she liked to feel his biceps. They indicated his strength. She saw that her caress was having the desired effect. He embraced her with a warm tenderness, his chest touching her breasts; he could hear the excited beating of her heart.

Next day, Ngurumo began the morning as usual. He was out at the second crow to feed the goats and the chickens. He walked around the farm; the maize was rippling and sighing in the wind.

When he returned to the house, Seitu had already prepared their first meal of the day. He sat down with her and ate. They had barely finished when they heard the mumble of human voices out in

72

the fields. Ngurumo rose up and went to the door.

Advancing towards the house with spears, bows and arrows in their hands were a number of men whom he immediately recognized. Ahead of them, and obviously their leader, was Fundi. Ngurumo sensed their hostility but it was already too late for him to return and snatch up a spear.

'What d'you want here?' he demanded.

No one replied. Instead, at a signal by Fundi, the men rushed on him. The first one was thrown down by Ngurumo but the struggle was too unequal to last long. Despite his valiant resistance, he was over-whelmed by their numbers. They tied his arms securely behind his back. Seitu had grabbed her baby and was shivering at the far side of the house.

'What are you doing?' Ngurumo asked as they raised him to his feet.

'You and your wife are to go back to Pachanga,' Fundi replied.

'We've no wish to go back,' Ngurumo said.

'The gods command you to be taken there.'

'What for? We've done nothing to offend the gods. Here they've greatly blessed us.'

'There's a curse on Pachanga until you return,' Fundi said.

Some of the men had taken hold of Seitu and were pushing her towards the doorway. Seeing this, Ngur-umo started to struggle again. Fundi stabbed the point of his spear into Ngurumo's arm. It was useless offering further resistance.

With Seitu carrying the baby and the men with point-ed spears and bows and arrows behind Ngurumo, his arms securely tied, they set out for Pachanga.

73

'What's to happen to us when we get back to the village?' Ngurumo inquired.

When they did not answer, his anxiety, already great, increased. He was worried about his fate but he was much more concerned for his wife and child. He was well aware of how cunning and cruel Mzee Matata could be. He knew that this was his doing. He was sure that they were not being taken to Pachanga simply to live there again as they had done in the past. The fetish priest had not gone to this trouble merely for that. There was something sinister in the whole exercise. Ngurumo's heart sank the more he thought of it. They went on in silence broken only by odd words and sentences exchanged between their captors. Nothing was said that threw light on why they were being taken back to Pachanga.

He kept looking at Seitu. She had a proud air about her as if she had a feeling of contempt for the men who had invaded their privacy and abducted them. Ngurumo was so filled with fear for her he felt a bitterness in his stomach that rose in sour heat into his throat.

He pondered over the whole unexpected invasion and capture. What had happened to cause Mzee Matata to have them brought back to the village? From the beginning of their escape from Pachanga, Ngurumo had feared that this might happen. As the days went by, he concluded that the fetish priest had decided to leave them in peace. Something had occurred which had caused him to change his mind. Ngurumo could not imagine what that could be.

There was no pause in the long journey to the village. The baby was crying and whimpering. The boy was

74

hungry. When they finally reached Pachanga, Seitu was staggering a little. Ngurumo was also feeling the effects of thirst and fatigue. He was taken to a hut and thrust inside it. Two guards were posted outside the door. Seitu and the baby were taken elsewhere.

'Why have we been brought here?' Ngurumo tried to find out.

The guards acted as if they had not heard him.

'Why have we been brought here?' Ngurumo asked again. 'We've done no wrong. We left the village because we saw there was too little food here. If we're to live, we need food. We started a new life out there on the Land of the East and it proved to be a good life. Anyone could have joined us there. There's room for all. There's abundance of food for all. Why have we been brought here?'

Still the guards behaved as though they had not heard him. This attitude increased Ngurumo's anxiety. The guards had been given strict orders not to speak to him. His fears were proving only too well founded. He knew that he and his wife – and perhaps their child as well – faced the gravest danger.

'If you harm us it'll do you no good,' he said. 'I led the way to a new life – a new life for all of us. You had only to follow. Am I to be punished for making a new start where there's the food we all need? If that offends the gods then do they want us to starve to death?'

There was no response from the guards.

'Whatever you do,' Ngurumo said further, 'don't harm my wife and child. They've done no wrong. Seitu has done only what I have told her to do. If anyone is to suffer, then let it be me alone. Don't harm them, I beg of you.'

75

The guards remained as impassive as dead wood.

'I'm thirsty,' Ngurumo shouted hoping this time to get their ears. 'Let me have water to drink.'

No one took any notice. Ngurumo knew that his doom was already sealed.

7   All day long, Ngurumo was kept a prisoner in the hut. Just before sunset, water was brought and poured into his mouth, but the thongs which so tightly bound his arms were not loosened. The guards were doubled. Mzee Matata, it was clear, was not taking any chances.

Ngurumo was in a desperate state of mind. He was so anxious about Seitu and the child that he could not have eaten even if food had been brought to him. He had long since ceased to struggle in an effort to free his arms. He knew that the bonds were too strong. Besides, it was impossible to escape with the armed guards around the hut. He and his whole family were at the mercy of Mzee Matata.

The night was very long. His fate filled him with dread but his heart was heavy for Seitu and the child. He felt he could die without regret for his actions if only they were spared to live. Dawn came at last. He was in a state of utter weariness. His eyes were gritty for lack of sleep. His arms ached because of the bonds securing them. He felt so weak that standing upright was an effort he could not make. Dawn brought no relief; rather it intensified the anxiety over his fate and that of his family. Very soon, he would face his executioners. He was sure his punishment would be terrible. He tried to keep calm but could not quieten the anxious beating of his heart. He could not quell the heat of the tension rising in waves from his stomach.

The guards were changed and again he was brought water but no food.

'Tell me what's to happen to me?' he asked the new guards.

They did not even glance over their shoulders.

'Tell me!' he begged them, 'I've done you no harm. Why should you refuse to talk to me?'

The guards remained as though they did not hear him. Ngurumo had a terrible urge to weep. Things had been going so well. He and Seitu were extremely happy. Life had been a joy and there had been plenty of food. They were more than content – fond of each other and of their child. That was all they asked of life as long as they lived. Then suddenly, without warning, everything had to change. They had been snatched from their home. Their maize would not be gathered, nor would their fruits. Their poultry and goats would go untended. The new house would rot until it collapsed.

As mid-morning approached, he heard sounds which suggested that the people were moving out of the village. This added to his anxiety. It suggested that some ceremony was about to be performed. He felt sure it concerned him.

'What's happening?' he asked the guards. 'You must tell me.'

Still they remained impassive.

'Tell me, tell me!' he cried out despairingly.

They would not say a word.

Their silence increased his anguish. There seemed to be something cruel in it. They had dismissed him as no longer one of themselves – excommunicated. The village was quiet. He guessed that it was deserted. Only he and the guards, he judged, were left in it. He would not be there for long. He heard the tramp of footsteps. Four more men joined the guards, each armed with a spear. Two of them entered the hut and took hold of him by the arms.

They pointed towards the doorway. Outside, two guards took up positions immediately in front of Ngurumo. Behind him came another group, with two men on each side. His nerves were at such a pitch, he felt like screaming to relieve the unbearable tension. He kept his lips tightly together. He walked with his head held high. There was a weakness in his legs. He had to walk with concentration to prevent himself from stumbling.

He noticed the burnt-out hut but did not understand its significance. He was led out of the village. He realized where he was being taken; soon he came in sight of the flat expanse of ground before the house of Mzee Matata. The people had already gathered. What he saw caused his whole body to chill as if it had been suddenly frozen.

Two stakes had been driven into the ground. Tied to one of them was Seitu. Guards had been positioned around her. There was no chance of her being able to run away. She had been tied very tightly at the ankles, legs, waist and shoulders. She had been separated from the child. Ngurumo sensed her anxiety.

78

She was gripped by a terror far greater than his own. He knew she had every reason to be afraid. He tried to give her a reassuring smile.

He was being tied to the stake beside Seitu when he saw the sacrificial stone. His eyes nearly leapt from their sockets. Stakes had been driven into the ground at each corner of the stone. This could mean only one thing.

'No, no, no!' he yelled. 'No – no – no!'

He heard the crowd murmur.

In an agony of fear, he looked round for their child. He was not in sight. Perhaps they did not intend to harm him. This brought him some comfort but it did not add to his courage. He knew the nature of the ordeal facing him. There was nothing that could save his and Seitu's lives.

Abedi emerged from the house of the fetish priest. Just behind him came Mzee Matata. In his hand he carried the sacrificial knife with a long, sharp two-edged blade. The handle was carved with images of the gods.

The expectation of the crowd increased as Mzee Matata made his regal progress. He halted and raised his arms. He said something which no one understood. It was addressed to the gods.

Ngurumo dared not look at his wife. He could not bear the sight of her anguish. His own terror was such he marvelled he did not faint.

'Men and women of Pachanga,' Mzee Matata began as usual. He lowered his arms and, with that grave and pompous air that was characteristic of him, continued his speech, 'as you know, the gods have been displeased with you for a long time. In our efforts to appease them, we have sacrificed chickens and goats. But the gods have not been satisfied.'

The crowd mumbled.

'These two people here,' pointing at Ngurumo and Seitu, 'are to blame. They have angered the gods and they preferred to run away, deserting their fatherland.'

He paused.

'The gods revealed their displeasure only two nights ago. They flung down from heaven the ball of fire which consumed one of our huts,' he reminded them. 'The gods have told me that the renegades had to be brought back. Their instructions were that Ngurumo and Seitu be offered as sacrifices.'

The place was silent. Ngurumo felt as if his legs had turned to water. Had he not been bound to the stake, he felt he would have fallen down.

'What's more,' the fetish priest said, 'the gods have ordered that they are to die as all animals are offered.'

A long roaring noise gushed forth. The people were about to witness the infliction of pain – the taking of human lives – and they were tingling with emotion that would intensify until it reached a pitch of ecstasy.

'These two have alienated themselves from us. By their own choice, they've separated themselves from us. Because of this the gods have decreed that they must die. The woman is to be sacrificed first.'

The people began to surge forward to have a better view of the ritual. The much awaited moment was near. Mzee Matata signalled to the guards. Immediately they cut the bonds holding Seitu to the stake. If they had not held her firmly, she would have fallen down. They carried her to the sacrificial stone and laid her on it. Then they tied her wrists and ankles to the stakes in the ground. She was now spreadeagled on the flat stone. Although she could convulse her body, she was quite unable to move her arms and legs.

Everybody knew what would happen the moment the fetish priest's sacred knife cut into her flesh. She would jerk violently. The knife, which would enter in the region of the stomach would be buried there for awhile. Then Mzee Matata would make a deep cut downwards right through the soft flesh of the belly; her blood and life would ebb as she writhed and cried in agony. After her, it would be Ngurumo's turn. By the time the knife was plunged into his belly, the whole assembly would be in a fever of sensuous excitement.

Ngurumo was suddenly possessed of a new surge of strength. He flung himself against his bonds, but they were much too strong for them to yield.

'Stop that! stop!' he screamed. 'You can't do that to Seitu. She's not. . . . '

He was silenced by Fundi who struck him a savage blow across the mouth. Ngurumo felt the blood seeping from his burst lips. He closed his eyes, not daring to look at what was about to take place.

The people around the stone closed in again forming almost a complete circle. The fetish priest, it seemed, had fallen into a trance. His eyes were glazed and he appeared to be looking into unfathomable deeps. Then he stepped forward to the stone on which Seitu lay, her eyes closed and her body shuddering as if with a high fever. He gestured and a guard unloosened the skirt around Seitu's waist. A jerk ripped it away. Apart from bangles and beads, she was naked.

The assembled people could not believe their eyes.

Nudity of children was common but there was something different in this. The woman was being deliberately exposed. And she happened to be a woman with an excellent figure. Besides, she had been stripped to be sacrificed.

The fetish priest raised his arms and extended them over her body. He began to offer what seemed to be the last prayers. His voice rose into a high pitch dying gradually into a low, indistinct sound. The hands of men were reaching out to women. Women were pressing their bodies against those of the men nearest to them. The pure morning air had suddenly been infected with an atmosphere of fear.

The incantation was over and it was time to make the sacrifice. Mzee Matata's eyes were now open. He selected the point at which the blade of the knife was to be driven into the body. The knife held aloft, he began to bring it down ceremoniously.

Suddenly, there was a shout followed by what sounded like an explosion. Something thudded into the chest of Mzee Matata. He sagged forward. The knife fell from his hand. Blood was oozing from a hole which had appeared in the left side of his chest. He fell to the ground. It was obvious that he was dying. Incredulously, everyone stood motionless until Mzee Matata was dead.

'Don't anyone move!' an unfamiliar voice commanded. It might have been the voice of the gods themselves.

Their own fetish priest – their leader and guide – had been struck dead before their own eyes. This really was a bolt from the sky. Only the gods could have done it. Nothing else could possess such a power.

Ngurumo, who had been steeling himself, eyes closed, for the sound of Seitu's screams, was the last to realize that something had happened. He opened his eyes. He stared incredulously. Mzee Matata lay in a crumpled heap beside the stone of sacrifice, blood still flowing from a wound in his chest. The fetish priest was dead. His wife was stretched out on the sacrificial stone but she was saved and so was he. He did not know why or how or by whom.

He began to weep for joy.

Part Two

8 'Stay where you are!'
The voice had such authority that no one
in the still shocked and bewildered assembly
attempted to move.

'Make way!'

At a point on the other side of the sacrificial stone
where Ngurumo had been tied to the stake, the
crowd parted. Through the opening strode a strange
and unfamiliarly dressed character. He wore a hat
with a broad brim. On the bridge of his nose and
linked to the ears were two transparent oval pieces
through which he blinked. These were his spectacles.
He was clothed in a two-piece of exotic shape in khaki.
The upper piece had two large pockets in front. The
lower piece had slit-pockets on both sides of the hips.
There were outer coverings of treated hide for the
feet up to the ankle. The people were not familiar with
such boots, nor with the puttees which they saw as
cloth strip wound round the legs from the ankle to
the knee.

He carried on his back a huge bag – a haversack –
hung from the shoulders. In his hand was what looked
like a sort of stick but this had a long, slender barrel
and a curiously shaped wooden end. It was the gun that
had killed Mzee Matata. Two other marvellous things
in leather casings were a pair of binoculars and a
camera. The first he explained to them later on as an
optical outfit for viewing objects at a distance and the
other as a gadget for copying the images of objects
when trained on them and manipulated.

The most curious thing he had with him was what
he was pushing. It had two large wheels on which it
moved. A seat and a curved handle were attached to its

frame. This – a bicycle – was the first thing on wheels any of the people of Pachanga had seen.

The man was thick set and had round, genial features. He had a moustache which he had kept well trimmed. His air was cheerful and confident. He raised his right hand and waved it in a sort of salute. Most of the people were already going down on their knees in obeisance.

'I'm no god. Keep upright,' he shouted sternly. He pointed at Seitu and then at Ngurumo. 'Release those two,' he ordered impatiently.

Nobody thought of defying him. One who came from nowhere and who could kill a powerful fetish priest from a distance was not one to be challenged. He was one to be obeyed instantly. A score of people rushed to set Ngurumo and Seitu free. When they were freed of their bonds, Ngurumo fell to the ground and Seitu was unable to sit upright.

'Bring water,' the stranger commanded.

Water arrived with a speed like lightning. Ngurumo drank greedily but he still felt numb and shaken. His heart beat with a fierce irregularity. The water did not fully revive him. However, it helped Seitu to sit up and reach for her clothing.

'A fetish priest, eh.' The stranger touched Mzee Matata with his boot. 'And one who offers human sacrifice. It's my bet that he's the last one on this island to pursue such heathen practices. He deserved to die.' He turned to the crowd.

'My name,' he announced, 'is Shabani. I've come from the town of Walata beyond the mountains.'

From his shoulders he removed the haversack and opened the flap. He brought out a roll of paper which

87

he spread into a broad wide sheet. It had some black marks on it. This was another object the people had not seen before. They could only stare in growing amazement. Shabani carefully laid it on the ground and then he placed stones at the four corners to prevent it from rolling back into its cylindrical form.

'Now,' he said, 'let me see.' He pointed to a spot on the map. 'We're on this island. Your village is not shown on it. Where we are is indicated simply as a wild and practically unpopulated swampy river basin. To the authorities, therefore, nobody lives here.'

He looked around him. He frowned as his gaze moved from one person to another.

'Underfed,' he said. 'All of you – all except you.' He pointed at Ngurumo. 'And you.' He pointed at Seitu. 'Can it be that they were fattening you two before they sacrificed you?'

'No,' replied Ngurumo, gradually recovering. 'We – Seitu and I – haven't lived here for some time. We were brought for Mzee Matata to sacrifice us to the gods.'

'Is that Mzee Matata?' Shabani indicated the fetish priest with his boot.

'That's right.'

'Well, there's no Mzee Matata now. Not that I meant to kill him, mind you. But I'm not a good marksman and I was in a hurry to prevent him from killing the beautiful young woman. I aimed at his knife hoping to knock it out of his hand. Unfortunately, I hit him right in the chest.' But Shabani showed no sign of regret for his action. He patted Ngurumo on the shoulder.

'Feeling better now?' he asked.

88

Ngurumo was overwhelmed by the timely action of his saviour. He was full of gratitude, but he simply stared at Shabani not knowing what to say. Seitu was still on the sacrificial stone. Friends were fussing about her, rubbing her wrist and leg wounds and consoling her.

'A shot of whisky will do you both good,' Shabani said hopefully. 'Just a minute.'

He dived his hand into the haversack again and this time brought out a transparent container which seemed to have in it lightly coloured water. He sought for a cup and poured some liquid into it. All these were strange things to the people. He took the cup to Seitu and placed it to her lips.

'Drink this,' he urged. 'It'll do you a great deal of good.'

Seitu tasted it, then she gasped and coughed. Shabani laughed.

'You're not used to it,' he said. 'Take it more slowly.'

By the time she had drunk the whole lot, she was beginning to show signs of recovery.

'There, what did I tell you?' Shabani said. 'Works like magic.'

He poured another generous measure for Ngurumo.

'Drink it slowly,' he advised. 'It'll make you feel like a new man.'

Ngurumo drank it cautiously. The liquid was not pleasant tasting, but it ran warmingly down his throat into his stomach. Shortly after emptying the cup he felt like his old self.

Seitu managed to get up and went to Ngurumo. Reaching him she burst into tears.

'Don't worry about that,' Shabani told Ngurumo. 'The poor woman has had a terrible ordeal. A cry will do her some good.'

He looked at the thing around his left wrist. 'Twelve-thirty,' he said and added, 'it's a time-piece.'

Aware of their curiosity, he began to explain the nature and advantages of a watch. Although many of them obviously did not understand him fully, a few, however, gathered his meaning.

'Time to eat,' Shabani said after he had carried the explanation of the watch as far as he could. From the haversack he took out food hermetically sealed in containers. As he opened them, the people looked on with ever increasing wonder.

'Look,' he said, his dark face glowing with humour, 'I'm a man, just like any other man. All these things you see are made by other human beings.'

Shabani had brought with him a cooker. The box of little sticks with the red tips which he had taken from his pocket seemed to work like magic. He just scraped the red tip on the side of the box and, lo, a flame appeared with which he lit the cooker to warm the food.

'You'd better tell me all about what was happening when I arrived this morning,' Shabani said.

Ngurumo recounted how he and Seitu came to be at Mzee Matata's mercy. As he unfolded the story, others helped him by adding a word here and there.

'This certainly beats anything I've come across before,' Shabani said after he had been told everything. 'And to think that there's somewhere in the world where people still sacrifice to gods to make things go right.' He shook his head in amazement. 'But you can't make anything grow by appealing to the gods.

Come, let's have a look at the land where your crops won't grow any more.'

They led him to a nearby field.

'Worked to death,' he said. 'Have you fertilised the land?'

Their blank expressions indicated that they did not know what he was talking about.

'Just like children,' he sighed. 'You think you can take out without putting in. It just can't be. You've grown crops on this soil for such a long time its freshness is lost. Ngurumo was right. He moved to a new and fertile land. Even there, later, unless the soil is manured or fertilised, the yields will reduce in quality and quantity each succeeding harvest. Land is like human beings; it has to be nourished or made to rest awhile.'

He looked around at the people rather ruefully. 'You've so much to learn.'

As if suddenly remembering him, he turned to Ngurumo and asked, 'What about your fetish priest?'

For the first time, Fundi spoke. Since Shabani's dramatic arrival, he had watched the stranger with such a mixture of fear and awe that he had not been able to find words.

'The fetish priest,' he said, 'must be buried in the sacred cemetery. The gods will be very angry if he's buried elsewhere.'

'How?' Shabani asked with incredulity. 'Had I not shot him at the time I did, he would have killed two innocent people – and in a most brutal and cruel manner. He doesn't deserve any sacred burial.'

'It's the gods who demand such a burial,' Fundi said stubbornly.

'And if he doesn't get such a burial?'

'Then evil will befall the tribe.'

'What sort of evil?'

'The crops won't grow and. . . .'

Shabani burst into a mocking laughter.

'Your crops haven't been growing well anyway,' he reminded Fundi. 'Don't blame the gods! Unless there's a drought, or floods, you must blame yourselves. Men have always blamed gods for their misfortunes. That's so much easier than trying to find the real cause of the trouble and then working to set things right.'

'Mzee Matata must be laid to rest in the sacred burying-place,' Fundi insisted.

'And I say he must be fed to the crocodiles,' Shabani replied.

Ngurumo realized that Shabani was not just trying to establish his authority. He was attacking beliefs which were obsolete.

Shabani made for where the dead fetish priest lay. It had been obvious from the very beginning that this stranger was a man of considerable strength. He had a well developed and well preserved frame with broad shoulders and muscular arms. He turned to Fundi.

'Would you say that your gods would strike me dead if I offended them?' he asked.

Fundi, nervous of this man, but hating him for interfering at a moment of vital importance, did not answer him.

'Your gods are all-powerful, aren't they? And the fetish priest was their intermediary. That being so, surely they'll strike me down if I don't treat him with respect?'

Fundi remained doggedly silent.

'Won't they?' Shabani demanded.

'Offend the gods and they'll destroy you,' Fundi replied.

'Then we'll put them to the test.'

Stooping, Shabani lifted up the body of Mzee Matata and raised it on to his shoulders. Flies, which had already found the carcase, rose buzzing.

'The flies don't show your fetish priest much respect,' he said.

He carried the body to the river. He waded in until he reached the deepest place. Taking a deep breath, he raised the body in both hands above his head and tossed it into the river. There was a big splash which attracted the crocodiles. They came swimming at a terrific speed. Shabani retreated to the bank without showing any sign of panic.

The people, greatly frightened, watched the water churning as the crocodiles fought to devour the body. Very soon, the water was calm again.

'That's the end of your Mzee Matata or whatever you called him,' Shabani said flippantly.

He turned to face Fundi.

'The gods must be very angry with me now. The bones of your fetish priest aren't resting at the sacred cemetery. They must be furious. And this is the moment for them to strike me dead.'

He looked up at the sky smiling in amusement. The blue sky remained undisturbed. Nothing happened.

'There you are, the gods don't seem to worry about their fetish priest. What's more, even about you. You have to rely on your own selves if you want to progress.'

'We've been working harder and harder but always for less reward,' Fundi spoke slowly but firmly. 'If the gods are angry. . . .'

'Forget about the gods.' Shabani smiled. 'It's useless working hard on a land that has become barren. It'll yield no more, no matter what you sacrifice to your gods. You have to learn from Ngurumo.'

'What's that?' asked Fundi.

'Move to the rich Land of the East. There you'll all have more than enough to eat.'

'We daren't do that,' protested Fundi. 'The land here is hallowed for us by the gods and. . . .'

'Who are you to tell the people what to do and what not to do?' Shabani interrupted.

'I'm Mzee Matata's successor,' Fundi retorted. 'He appointed me to be the new fetish priest and ruler if he should die.'

Shabani chuckled.

'That was very good of Mzee Matata. No doubt by doing that he made sure he had you as an ally. You can't *make* yourself the new ruler, especially as you intend to go on keeping the people here in subjection, and tied to a land on which they're bound to starve to death.'

'Then who is to rule?' Fundi asked.

'I think the people themselves will have to decide that.'

'The people? How?'

'It's quite simple. Let them have their first lesson in democracy. They'll vote to choose the new ruler.'

It took Shabani a long time to explain what he meant by democracy and voting. At last, he showed

94

the adults how to make different marks on paper he had with him. He did it using a stick which made black marks on the paper.

'A pen. It's called a pen,' Shabani held aloft the thing that scribbles for all to see.

'The people must vote for me,' Fundi said. 'That's what the gods decree.'

'The people themselves will decide,' replied Shabani. 'I agree you can be one of the candidates. Ngurumo I would suggest as another.'

He turned to Ngurumo.

'You've shown yourself to have initiative and intelligence. You went on your own to a new land and you made a success there. If you can do it for yourself, you should be able to do it for others. Are you willing to stand?'

Ngurumo thought for a while. Then he gave his assent. Fundi scowled darkly.

'Very well, we now have Fundi and Ngurumo as candidates. Does anyone else wish to contest?'

No one signified that he did.

'Then we'll arrange a poll for you to decide who's to be your new leader. But first of all we'll take a look at the Land of the East,' Shabani said to Ngurumo. 'I would like to see what you made of it.'

Ngurumo looked at Shabani. He had powers no one guessed existed. But he was no god. Here was a man who knew much, much more than themselves. He had marvellous things and one of them could even kill from a distance. Ngurumo did not know where these things came from but he wondered if there could not be such things for the people of Pachanga. Supposing they could be brought to the people or made by them.

95

It was such an exciting thought Ngurumo felt it just could not be made to come true.

'Will you take me to your new home?' Shabani asked Ngurumo.

'Gladly. But what about my wife, Seitu?'

'Will she be all right if we leave her here?'

'I think so. Let me ask her wishes.'

Ngurumo looked for Seitu. She was sitting in the sunshine, nursing their child. She looked much better but she had not fully recovered from her ordeal.

'Seitu,' he called her. 'The man who saved us from Mzee Matata has expressed the desire to see our new home in the east. The animals will be very hungry and should be fed. Will you be all right here until I return tomorrow? I think you need some rest before you can make the journey.'

Seitu seemed uncertain but she conceded.

'You can go, my husband, but when shall we both be returning to the new home?'

'As soon as we're back. It will not be long.'

Before they left, Ngurumo had a last minute chat with his old friend, Bakari.

'Take care of Seitu and my child for me, will you?' he said patting him on the back. 'All being well, Shabani and I will be back tomorrow.'

'They'll be all right with me,' Bakari promised.

'I'm sure they will,' Ngurumo replied.

9 Ngurumo and Shabani emerged from the jungle. In front of them spread the undulating rich land on which Ngurumo and his wife had made their new home. Standing still with both hands firm on his hips, Shabani looked intently over the tall, thick grass.

'You did well to come here. What caused you to move?' he asked.

'The fact that we were always hungry,' Ngurumo replied.

'But how did you know that food would grow well here when it didn't in Pachanga?'

'It just occurred to me that if grass grew richly here, maize and other crops would grow likewise.'

'You aren't without vision.' Shabani looked at the figure standing before him. 'I like your high forehead; that testifies rare intelligence. Those bold eyes of yours – they suggest perception. And the fact that you came all this long distance shows that you have initiative and you're enterprising.'

Shabani turned round to look across the plain towards the mountains. He nodded approvingly.

'Now, let's have a quick look around the farm you've made and then the house you've built.'

They began to walk on to the plain, over the footpath Ngurumo and Seitu had trodden almost to their death only two days before. They had not gone far, however, when from somewhere in the high grass ahead of them they heard gruntings which warned them that some animals were foraging across their path.

'Rhinos,' Shabani whispered to Ngurumo.

'Then we'd better take care,' Ngurumo whispered back.

They moved on but cautiously. They came close to a spot where the grass had been trampled down. They saw three rhinos. One was so small it could not have been more than a few moons old. The parents, particularly the male, were large. Like Shabani, Ngurumo knew that rhinos despite their ponderous motion, were capable of considerable speed when pursuing an enemy.

'If we make a detour, we shall have to push through the grass. I don't fancy that's good in this heat,' said Shabani.

'We can go ahead along the same path keeping a careful eye on them.'

'Be ready to run if they show signs of charging. That male looks dangerous to me.'

They went on, warily watching the browsing rhinos. Unfortunately, the wind was against them, and both male and female were lifting their heads and sniffing the air suspiciously.

Ngurumo and Shabani approached them cautiously, Shabani with his gun at the ready and Ngurumo his spear poised in his hand.

'We shouldn't aim at them unless we're absolutely forced,' Shabani said in a low voice.

The female rhino raised its head, smelling the air. Then it looked towards the two men. They halted, but the rhino lowered its head and began to charge.

'Run for dear life!' Shabani shouted.

Ngurumo showed himself to be a faster runner than his companion. Suddenly, he heard a gasp and a thud behind him. Shabani had tripped over a log and had fallen down, his gun lying away from him. The rhino was bearing down on the sprawling Shabani with unusual speed. The ground was shaking as it approached.

The rhino was only some ten arm-lengths from Shabani when Ngurumo threw his spear. It was well aimed. The poisoned tip bit into the left eye, finding one of the few vulnerable regions in the animal's body. It made a few more strides and then it stumbled. A terrible squeal followed as its head jerked forward. It rolled over on its back in agony. Then it shuddered violently from nose to tail and slowly toppled over on to its side, dead.

Shabani, already up on his feet, fetched his rifle. It was a good thing he did so quickly. The male rhino, aroused by what had happened, was also charging. The female had looked formidable but the male was worse.

Calmly, Shabani went down on one knee, raised the rifle to his eye level and trained the muzzle on the head of the animal as it approached snorting. He squeezed the trigger. There was an explosion. The rhino seemed to jump into the air. A loud crack followed. The plunge down to earth had broken its neck.

Ngurumo and Shabani looked at each other in mutual astonishment. Slowly Shabani rose to his feet.

'You saved my life,' he said.

'Then I've merely repaid you for saving mine,' Ngurumo retorted. 'And for saving my wife's as well.'

'That was nothing,' said Shabani. 'Mzee Matata was obviously good only for death. He has held the people of Pachanga back far too long, all for his own profit and aggrandisement. A ruler who sacrifices human beings has certainly outlived this age. I've no regrets for killing Mzee Matata.'

They moved towards Ngurumo's house and enclosures.

When Shabani saw the house that Ngurumo had built and all that he had done, he said: 'You've done well, but if the house were made of wood, it wouldn't harbour insects like reeds and mud do.'

Ngurumo listened attentively. He had not thought of such a thing.

'You have to learn how to make the land yield without exhausting the soil,' Shabani continued. 'That calls for rotation of crops as we call it. It means you grow one kind of crop on a plot one season and another kind the next season. You also have to fertilize the soil. Let the animals feed on one part of the land for a period and then on the next part. Cattle are what you need primarily for this purpose. Large tracts can be cleared for cattle grazing. Land which has been used to grow food must be allowed to go back to grass and to rest for a while. Cattle can graze on it and they'll fertilize it while doing so. You also need something else.'

'What's that?' Ngurumo asked. He wanted to know more from the man who had all the attributes and powers of a god but who yet was not god.

'Your staple diet has been maize. It's good but by no means enough. You may need some seed potatoes.'

'Potatoes?'

'Yes. They're tubers and they yield ten, twenty and even thirty fold and can be cooked in many different ways. They go well with meat, fish and vegetables.'

'You mean we'll get them for nothing?'

'Why not?' Shabani laughed. 'After all, when I tell the people of Walata living beyond the mountains from where I came about my discovery and of the problems and difficulties you face, there's no doubt that they'll be willing to give you some help.'

Shabani told the surprised Ngurumo that he and his people were but a small part of a big race inhabiting an island. They were in the hinterland, surrounded by mountains. They had been cut off from the rest by the remoteness of Pachanga and by the absence of any road joining it to other towns. Moreover the village was cordoned off almost half the year by a barrier of floods. During the dry season, the risk of penetrating the jungle infested with man-eating mammals and walking the long distance he had covered over the mountains, down valleys, through impassable swamps and fording knee-deep rivers was enormous.

'Don't be surprised if I speak your language for we're of the same stock. Only circumstances have brought about your isolation,' Shabani concluded his long explanation.

Ngurumo was baffled by what he had heard. His people had always felt that Pachanga was all the world. The horizon was the limit. They were the only people under the sun. Ngurumo was amazed at the amount of knowledge Shabani had and was wondering why people of his kind knew about so many things and why the people of Pachanga were in their miserable condition.

'I'm going to write all about you in a book and. . . . '

'A book?'

Shabani tried to explain what a book was. When he had finished he felt he had not altogether succeeded.

'Anyway,' he said, 'there'll be pictures in the book.'

'Pictures?'

Again, Shabani did some explanation. He had left his camera back in Pachanga and he could not show Ngurumo any of the pictures he had already taken.

'I'll show you what I mean when we return to Pachanga,' he said when he noticed that Ngurumo was not following the conversation. 'I shall be paid for my book and for newspaper and magazine and radio rights. I shall also. . . . '

Shabani stopped speaking abruptly after realizing that his words meant nothing to Ngurumo. They were passing by him like the wind itself.

'I seem to be far ahead of myself,' Shabani said apologetically. 'You must forgive me. I'm so used to these things, I find it hard to fancy you haven't any idea about what I'm talking. In any case, they're not important. What does matter is how you can make good use of this rich land.'

The topic changed to how the land could be properly tilled, the value of irrigation and bringing water through canals from the stream to the farm. Ngurumo then showed him the canal he had made to carry away refuse.

'That's splendid but you can do better than this. I saw in Pachanga how hundreds of flies were drawn there by the refuse allowed to lie where the people had thrown it. You should bury your refuse. That way it won't attract flies. And you'll protect your health too. For flies carry germs – the germs which make people ill.'

'Germs?' Ngurumo repeated. 'What are germs?'

'They're very dangerous living creatures. They are so small you can't see them with your naked eyes. They spread diseases of many kinds. They breed in refuse.

Flies pick up the germs and carry them sometimes on to your food and you become ill after eating.'

'Mzee Matata said it was the gods which caused illness and disease.'

'I'm sure he would because he was ignorant,' Shabani said with great emphasis. 'But you'll see that there's much less disease if you bury the refuse and so make it impossible for flies to get to it.' Then he asked: 'What d'you do when you fall sick?'

'We used to go to Mzee Matata and he gave us herbs and powders. Sometimes, he offered prayers to the gods to cure the ailment.'

'I can imagine how much good the prayers did. What about the herbs and powders? Did they help?'

'Often they proved to be good but not always. There were times when the herbs didn't work at all and people died. We've lost many people in one round of sickness.'

'That would be due to an outbreak of an epidemic but it can be prevented. What you need to do is to make sure the food you eat and the water you drink are pure. If they're not, people fall ill. You've much to learn. I'll talk with the authorities when I get back to Walata, and see whether they can send you a man who makes sick people well. We call him a doctor. He'll show you how to avoid many of the diseases which afflict your tribe.'

Shabani talked of many other things and a great deal also about what he called education. It all meant to Ngurumo a sort of magic. Through education, Shabani said, they could learn about nature, how to become healthy and live longer.

By the time the day was over, Ngurumo had heard

of so many novelties that thoughts chased one another through his head. His mind was in a whirl. Shabani had not stopped talking even when Ngurumo was feeding the goats and the chickens and collecting the eggs; not even when they were eating their evening meal together. It was confusing, but there was one thing, however, which Ngurumo would not forget.

'You're the right man to be the leader of your people,' Shabani told him. 'You're the only one with the intelligence and enterprise to be their Moses.'

'Who's Moses?' Ngurumo asked.

'He led his people out of bondage,' Shabani explained. 'That's what you must do for your people. They're not the slaves of a nation or people; they're the slaves of ignorance, superstition and outworn ideas and beliefs. They have to be persuaded to come and begin a new life here.'

'That was what I told them many moons ago.'

'And now they have to do it. There's nothing they can gain from where they are. They have robbed the land of its life-giving properties. Only a few fish remain in the river in that stretch over there. Oh! yes, my friend, you have to start all over again. Pass on to them the information I've given to you.'

'But you yourself have made it impossible for me to do this.'

Shabani was a little taken aback by Ngurumo's remarks.

'How have I done that?' he asked.

'You told the people to choose their leader. What if they choose Fundi?'

'Why d'you think they'll do that?'

'Because they didn't take my advice about starting

a new life here. They preferred to remain hungry rather than follow me.' He indicated the land that spread so splendidly away to the foot of the mountains. 'All this was here waiting for them to come and claim it. But they stayed behind although they were starving.'

'You've reminded me of something I ought not to have forgotten. People often prefer to remain where they are, doing what they've always done, no matter how foolish and harmful it is. You're quite right, they may well prefer Fundi as their leader. That's the kind of thing that has happened again and again. Men have chosen leaders who have led them to disaster. If the people of Pachanga do elect Fundi, he'll certainly tighten the old fetters around them. He'll hold them captives to their ignorance, superstition and fears. And they'll remain in Pachanga until they're too feeble to move, and so they will perish.'

'That's what I fear will happen unless you tell the people that I'm to be their new leader. . . . '

'Oh, no! that's not democracy. It's dictatorship and that can only lead to trouble. All we can do is to rely on the good sense of the people.'

Ngurumo looked depressed. If Fundi were in charge of the people of Pachanga, he would destroy Seitu and himself just as Mzee Matata had meant to do. There would be no room for them to survive.

'There's one thing you can do for me as a favour,' he said.

'What's that?'

'Tell the people to make me their leader.'

'I can't do that. They'll have to make up their own

minds. I'm sure they'll choose you because they see you're a better man than Fundi.'

Ngurumo did not understand why Shabani was taking that attitude. After all, it was vital to the future and the very existence of the people that they should not elect Fundi as their ruler. He would lead them astray.

'You see, if the people don't choose you themselves, they won't accept you if you're imposed on them. If it's Fundi they want, they can find a way to have him.'

'And even if the people do decide to have me as their ruler, Fundi may want to overthrow me.'

'Knowing that, you can be ready for him.'

'Ready with spears? Is that what you mean?'

'Yes, if that becomes necessary. But I really mean that you take measures to make it impossible for a rebellion to succeed.'

'How can I do that?'

'You need a cabinet.'

'A thing like yours for defence?' Ngurumo pointed at the gun.

Shabani burst into laughter.

'No, no!' he said. 'It's not a weapon of any kind. It means that you share the rule of your people with other men whom you yourself choose.'

The light of confidence appeared in Ngurumo's eyes.

'It's an excellent idea. Then I can't be overthrown without the rest.'

'That's right. You have friends, I'm sure. Bring them into your cabinet to help you to rule. They'll give you advice, warn you of what your enemies are doing and tell you what the people need. But each man will have to look after one thing. For example, one man may look after farming and its problems and another may take care of the sanitation of the village and so on.'

'They will have to learn about these things.'

'That's what I've been saying all day. Education! It's what you and your people need to make life happy. But there's no one here to teach you and there can be no education without teachers.'

'Won't you be able to do the teaching?' Ngurumo asked.

'Only for a few days. I can't stay longer. You see, I must explore the other lesser known parts of the island.' Shabani explained again to Ngurumo that where the people of Pachanga were living was only a very tiny part of a large island. He told him of black men, white men, brown men and yellow men living together on other parts of it in towns and cities many times bigger than Pachanga.

He also mentioned what seemed quite incredible wonders. Of man-made structures which moved over the ground at a hundred miles an hour or more. This meant little to Ngurumo as he did not know what an hour was nor did he know what a mile was. But he did grasp the fact that what Shabani called motor cars were driven by their own power. Shabani spoke, too, of ships that were like floating villages and carried large numbers of people over wide stretches of water. Then he talked of something which took to the air carrying men and women at terrific speed.

'Ah,' said Ngurumo, 'we've seen that sort of thing like a bird before.'

'Really? You mean flying overhead?'

'Yes, one came down not far from the village. We

went to look at it but we did not dare to touch it.'

'Crashed, eh?' Shabani was anxious to know more but Ngurumo did not know why it fell from the skies. Mzee Matata had explained that the gods destroyed the creatures in it.

Shabani kept on talking, telling him of more of the wonders of the world. Ngurumo by no means understood all that his companion was telling him, but he did realize that his people were doing things in a way which all other peoples had abandoned long since.

'It must be a marvellous world, the one you come from.'

'In some ways it is – very marvellous indeed. But some of the people in it are not happy.'

'Not happy!' Ngurumo could hardly believe that Shabani was serious.

'Far from happy,' was the reply. 'They sometimes take their own lives.'

'Kill themselves!' This was something Ngurumo found it hard to believe. He had never known anyone who had destroyed himself. 'Why, everyone struggles all the time to keep alive here, and there's much weeping when a man or a woman is eaten by a crocodile or a lion, or dies of disease.'

'I know,' Shabani nodded sombrely. 'But you mustn't think that all the people in my world are unhappy. Most of them, I would say, very much enjoy themselves.'

When the two men finally settled down for the night, Ngurumo's mind was so full of new knowledge of the world with its mysteries and miracles, he was unable to sleep for quite some time.

The next morning, after breakfast with Shabani,

.Ngurumo fed the goats and the chickens. He put aside extra food in case he was not back the same day with his family.

Then they set off for the return journey to Pachanga.

10 In Pachanga, Fundi had been busy. His subtle and devious mind had been quick to see that his position was gravely threatened. During the reign of Mzee Matata, he had enjoyed several privileges; he had also been assured that he would become the next ruler as soon as the fetish priest had gone to the land of the gods. Now, it seemed his hopes for power would not materialize and he was going to lose the privileges too. The arrival of Shabani had numbed him.

All night, Fundi lay awake thinking of what he could do to ensure that he became Mzee Matata's successor. He was not without friends. There was Abedi, for instance, who had worked for Mzee Matata as his secret agent. There was Salifu, who had seen the wisdom in identifying himself with the fetish priest. Above all, there was Zamani. She was ruthless and unscrupulous.

Shabani had said that a new leader would be chosen by the people. This had never been done before. The fetish priest named his successor and then the installation ceremony was performed after he had died. Mzee **Matata** had not named anyone to succeed him because he had been killed unexpectedly. But everyone knew that he would have named Fundi had he lived to name anybody.

It was obvious, however, that Shabani exercised a great influence on the people as long as he was with them. There were those who still regarded him as a god. It was true he had strange and frightening powers. He could kill even a fetish priest by pointing a stick at him from a distance. The stick spat and at the same moment something entered the body of the victim killing him instantly.

Fundi felt nervous when he thought of how Mzee Matata had died. If Shabani could kill the fetish priest like that then he could kill anyone in the same manner. Nevertheless, Fundi had so set his heart on power he was unwilling to see the prize snatched from him. It pained him to think that Ngurumo would almost certainly become the ruler of the people. That thought inflamed him like a fever and bred in him a deepening hatred.

Before dawn, he had devised a plan. As soon as the first meal of the day had been eaten, he called Abedi, Salifu and Zamani secretly into his hut.

Salifu was fat and would have been fatter had there not been a shortage of food over the past moons. He liked the good things of life, and he found it fit to identify himself with the man in power if he was to enjoy them. That was why he had always been, like Fundi and Abedi, one of Mzee Matata's menials.

Zamani, on the other hand, was lean and well-built. Although she had three children, she still looked surprisingly young. However, there was something strange about her and everyone was frightened of her.

Occasionally she was seized by an ungovernable rage. When that happened, her family and friends and particularly her husband tried to keep out of her way.

'I've called you here,' Fundi began, 'because we must outwit Ngurumo. If we don't, he'll become the new ruler.'

'Did the powerful stranger not say that the people are to choose the man who is to be our leader?' Salifu asked.

'That's so,' Fundi answered. 'You know too well that they'll choose Ngurumo if we don't get rid of him.'

'No doubt they will,' Zamani said. 'I don't like to see it.'

'I don't like it either,' Salifu said.

'Nor do I,' Abedi agreed. 'But I don't see how we can prevent it. This Shabani obviously supports Ngurumo. That will influence the people a great deal. He has great powers and he has shown the people many wonders.'

'I'm aware of all this,' Fundi said rather impatiently, 'but we too can produce wonders. Haven't I the ears of the gods?'

'How can you have, before you're made a fetish priest?' Salifu asked him.

Fundi looked at his companions craftily. 'D'you remember when the sparks of fire fell from the sky and burned out one hut?'

They did.

'Well, it was I who produced that magic,' Fundi revealed.

'You?' They stared at him in astonishment.

'Yes. The gods showed me how to go about it. What's

111

more they want me to do that again – only this time on a larger scale.'

'Can we be of any help?' Zamani asked.

'Listen carefully and I'll tell you what to do.'

Fundi told them in detail how the first fire had been organized and thrown on the hut that burned to ashes. He then went on to tell them of his new plan.

'It's a clever idea,' Salifu said. 'We'll help you in the way you have directed us.'

'Sooner or later, the stranger will go away. Then we shall have the sacrifice that he denied us,' Fundi assured them.

'You mean Ngurumo and Seitu will be offered as sacrifice?' Zamani asked.

'Exactly,' replied Fundi. 'Mzee Matata was right. We haven't prospered during the last many moons because we've failed to offer the gods the human sacrifices they require. Our forefathers used to offer one maiden and one swain before sowing time. And look how well they lived. The land yielded richly and so did the river. But there came a fetish priest who claimed the gods no longer required human sacrifices. Since then our fortunes have declined. Mzee Matata before his untimely death was determined to resuscitate the old custom by offering the gods a man and a woman in order to regain their regard.'

When the three left the hut, they did so stealthily, hoping they had not been observed.

The work of the day was over. People were eating their evening meals when sparks of fire began to shower down upon the village. They seemed to leap out of the empty sky. The people were so alarmed by what was happening that they did not bother to find out the source of the fire. Their gaze remained riveted on the sparks which were falling on some of the hut roofs. As many as six of them were soon alight. The people, terrified, dashed to the outskirts of the village, the women snatching up their children. Seitu and her child went with them. There was nothing to explain the sudden shower of fire. This could only mean that the gods were angry with the people. And there was no hope of saving the huts that had caught fire.

Before long, the huts were burnt, leaving only charred and acrid smelling heaps of smouldering debris. The people looked anxiously skywards, fearing another shower of fire. Darkness was falling, and Fundi called all the people together.

'The gods are very angry with you,' he told them, resorting to the tactics that had been used so long and so often to impress them. 'You've given hospitality to a stranger who is not welcome to them. You've shown friendliness to a man who killed your fetish priest and ruler. You've listened to one who has told you to select your new leader; and you know it is the gods who decide who's to be your guide and leader.'

There was a brief silence. Near Fundi stood Abedi, Salifu and Zamani. The silence was broken by Bakari, Ngurumo's friend

'And who's to be our new ruler?' he asked boldly. 'Would it be you, Fundi?'

'That's what the gods decree. Mzee Matata told me many times that the gods had decided that I was the one they had chosen to follow him when the time came. That time has come.'

'Then you mean to challenge the stranger? You must

113

be very sure of yourself to do that. For Shabani is very powerful. He has the stick that kills when he points it at you.'

Everyone sensed the tension between the two men. Bakari was Ngurumo's closest friend. The stranger's remarkable powers and his apparent miraculous arrival were still fresh in their minds. But they had also been impressed by the sparks of fire which had burned down the huts. They were too steeped in superstition and ancient beliefs to be able to shake them off easily.

'I've no need to challenge the stranger,' Fundi said. 'You must choose me as your leader. Do that and the stranger can't harm you. If you fail to do so the gods will be angry and they'll destroy not only your homes with fire but you yourselves.'

'The stranger and Ngurumo will be back tomorrow,' Bakari reminded him. 'The decision about who's to be the new leader can't be taken until then.'

'You've already been warned,' Fundi pointed out. 'The gods have spoken. The soul of Mzee Matata has now joined those of our forefathers. It's he who has added his voice to theirs, and that's why the fire was unleashed.'

No one spoke, and Fundi was satisfied.

'Would those whose huts weren't destroyed by the gods offer rooms to the victims?' he pleaded. 'Tomorrow, we'll rebuild theirs.'

*　　*　　*

Ngurumo and Shabani were back the following afternoon. They found the people in a state of consternation. The smell of burning still lingered in the air. Men and women were busy building new huts.

'Oh, Ngurumo,' Seitu exclaimed, running up to him, 'something terrible has happened. Fire descended from the heavens on the village. Many huts have been destroyed.'

Shabani looked at her intently.

'You mean that the fire fell from the sky?' he asked.

'That's what happened. It poured down in sparks.'

'You had a storm. Was there thunder and lightning?'

'There was no storm. The sky was quite clear but the fire came,' Seitu replied.

Shabani looked a bit perplexed.

'That can't be,' he said. 'Fire doesn't fall from the skies.'

'But fire did fall from the heavens. I saw it myself. Everybody saw it.'

Shabani rubbed his chin thoughtfully with his right palm.

'There must be some explanation.'

'There is. It was the gods who sent down the fire.'

'The gods? Who pumped this idea into your head, Seitu?'

'Fundi said the gods sent down the fire because we've listened to you.'

'And the gods don't want you to listen to me?'

'That's what he said, Shabani.'

'There's more in it than meets the eye. Tell me, Seitu, how did the people react to Fundi's claim?'

'They agreed that it was because they had offended the gods that the fire came down from the sky.'

'But just how have I upset the gods?'

'Fundi said that the gods don't approve of the

people choosing their leader. The gods themselves make the choice.'

'I see. And I suppose the leader the gods have chosen is Fundi himself?'

'He said so.'

'The fire was a trick,' Shabani said confidently.

Ngurumo listened to the conversation in growing uneasiness.

'But it did come,' he said. 'And as Seitu tells us, the people were very much impressed.'

'Yes, that was the purpose of the fire,' Shabani said. 'Fundi schemed it to woo the people. It's a determined effort to win power. What's more, it's one that might well succeed.'

Ngurumo looked at him.

'D'you really think Fundi arranged the fire?'

'I'm sure that was his handiwork. We had better have the election as soon as we can. The choice of the new leader must be made while I'm here. Obviously, Fundi is very clever and cunning and he's determined to be the new ruler. I must show that I possess greater magical powers.'

'How d'you propose to do that?' Ngurumo asked.

'Call all the people together at the meeting place. Tell them they're to see magic they've never seen before.'

It did not take long for the people to assemble. With Ngurumo and Seitu beside him, Shabani took up a position on the stone of sacrifice.

'I've already shown you some magic. Now I'll show you more. The gods have armed me with greater powers. For instance, they've made it possible for me to eat fire. Watch!'

116

From a packet he took out a small roller-shaped, white-covered object and held it with his lips. He struck one of the sticks with the red tips against the side of the container. He lit the cigarette and began to blow. Smoke poured out in a thick jet from his mouth and through his nose in two streams.

The people stared at him in amazement. Taking the cigarette from his mouth, Shabani turned to where Fundi was standing.

'Perhaps you can eat fire like that?' Shabani suggested. He held out the cigarette. But Fundi, looking very uncomfortable, refused to take it.

'It's quite easy.'

Shabani went on smoking. The people were so stupefied by what seemed to them fire-eating that almost all present gasped for breath. Then Shabani addressed Fundi again.

'I'm sure you can eat fire, too. Such a simple magic isn't beyond you.'

Fundi was in an acute state of anxiety. He knew all eyes were turned on him, waiting to see how he reacted to the test. It was one he dared not refuse.

'Yes, if Shabani can eat fire, then I can also eat it.'

He strode to where Shabani was standing, his face showing no emotion. Shabani handed the cigarette to Fundi. Fundi hesitated. The intently watching crowd left him no choice. Opening his mouth, he pushed in the lighted end. As the burning tip touched his tongue, he let out a howl of pain. He spat the cigarette out. In the attempt, he burnt his lips and the side of his cheeks.

Shabani laughed loudly at Fundi's failure.

'So you don't have the same magical powers as I

have,' he teased Fundi. 'I've greater powers than I've yet shown you. I can make a man look ten times taller than he is.'

He held out his pair of binoculars.

'Look at a man, a woman, a tree or anything through the two transparent holes and you'll find them many times bigger than their usual size.'

It took him some time before he could persuade anyone to try it. Eventually, one young man agreed to peep through. He cried out in astonishment, his eyes bulging in amazement.

'It's true,' he screamed. 'It's true. Everything looks much bigger.'

As one after another looked through the binoculars, there were squeals of surprise and cries of unbelief. Fundi was one of the last to look. His mouth was still hurting him from the burns. Inwardly, he was raging furiously against Shabani but he had to see what the binoculars could do. He could not conceal his astonishment.

'There's more magic than you've known,' Shabani told the people. 'If you look through from the other end, the objects you see shrink in size and are very far away.'

This time, the people were so eager to try it was a problem deciding who was to be the first and the second and so on. This was indeed magic. For here was something which expanded men to many times their usual size and yet the same thing could shrink men to the size of infants.

Shabani called the meeting to attention and then he began to address the people.

'I've shown you that the gods are with me. They've

given me great powers. It's the gods which tell me that you must start your lives afresh, away from here on the Land of the East. There you'll live in prosperity. It was Ngurumo who showed you the way, but you didn't follow him. Ngurumo was right and wise. His crops are rich and bounteous. The land there is kind and generous. It'll give happiness to those who live there. Before you go there, you'll have to choose your new leader. You'll do so the day after tomorrow. The choice is between Ngurumo and Fundi. It's not for me to tell you who you should choose. You'll have to decide that yourselves.'

Ngurumo felt disappointed and discouraged. He had expected Shabani to advise the people to vote for him. Ngurumo was sure he would win easily if Shabani had done so.

'Remember that if you choose Fundi you'll remain here, living as you've always done in poverty and hunger. But if you choose Ngurumo, you'll live a new life of prosperity on the new land,' Shabani told the people. His gaze moved from face to face wondering if they understood him. 'Tomorrow, both Ngurumo and Fundi will have the chance to speak to you here. Each of them will say why you should make him the new ruler. Having heard them, you'll elect the man you want the following day.'

The meeting was over. The people began to return to their huts. Ngurumo was still not happy with Shabani's neutrality.

'You should have told them to choose me. Your word is a command to the people and they would certainly obey you.'

'My friend, you're mistaken. If I had told them who

to vote for, then I would have chosen the new ruler and not the people themselves. They've got to make the choice themselves. I shall be surprised if you don't win.'

Ngurumo, however, was not sure. He knew that the people had been greatly impressed by Shabani's display of magic but he also felt that some of them were reluctant to make any change in their way of life.

As they walked back to the village, Shabani discussed the fire with Ngurumo.

'There must be an explanation for it. It wasn't lightning. It couldn't have been a fallen meteor: they rarely strike the earth in showers and certainly don't come at one's convenience. I would very much like to find out how Fundi did it.'

After a meal, he set out with his gun and his binoculars. Ngurumo went with him. Clear of the village and in no danger of being overheard, Shabani said, 'Fundi is a very clever man. He had most cleverly tricked the people.'

'How has he done that?' Ngurumo asked.

'By making the sparks of fire.'

Ngurumo looked at Shabani unbelievingly.

'How could he have done it?' he asked.

'It isn't too difficult. Bind together, say, the fallen and dry branches of a palm tree. Light the torch and take it up a tree. Climb as high as you can. Make sure you're on the windward side of the village. Shake the torch violently. The wind will carry the shower of sparks to the village. Anyone seeing the sparks will take it that they're descending from the sky. This is what was done. The fire was not from the gods but from the cunning hands of Fundi or one of his cronies.'

The explanation convinced Ngurumo but he was not so sure the people would accept it.

'How can you prove what you're saying?' he posed.

'By finding traces of burning or scorching in a tree,' was the answer.

'But you can't climb all the trees around the village – that's impossible.'

'I've no need to do so.' Shabani patted the case containing his binoculars. 'These will magnify the tree tops so much so that I can see them as clearly as if I'm high in their branches.'

Nevertheless, in spite of a careful survey of the tops of several possible trees, he failed to find the evidence he sought.

'I should have known that Fundi is too crafty,' he said. 'He has too much at stake to risk leaving any evidence.'

'You're still convinced that it was Fundi who caused the shower of fire?'

'Does that mean that you're not?'

Ngurumo was silent. He just scratched his head.

'It's not easy for you to break away from old beliefs and ideas,' said Shabani. 'If it's hard for you to accept my explanation, then I don't know how much more difficult it will be for the others. You've shown yourself eager to adopt new ideas. The rest lack your enterprise and brightness. Persuading them to adopt a new way of life is going to be very hard indeed.'

'D'you think it's impossible?'

'Oh, no! In this world nothing is impossible,' Shabani said emphatically.

'Nothing at all?' Ngurumo repeated.

'Nothing at all,' Shabani affirmed. 'Men have shown

121

themselves able to travel right round the world in a few days. They've explored the bed of the sea. They've split the atom and released its power, although an atom is something no one has ever seen. People who can do these and so many other marvellous things, can do any-thing – anything. But I must admit that the hardest thing for most people is to discard outworn beliefs and ideas.'

'You think the beliefs of the people of Pachanga are outdated?'

'Certainly they are.'

11 The next day the people assembled to hear Ngurumo and Fundi each stating why he should become the new leader. Ngurumo spoke first. It was a short speech but it carried weight.

'I'll lead you to a new land and a new life,' he promised. 'It's a genial and fertile land. There we can know only prosperity and plenty, there we shall build better houses and have more of all the things we need. I shall rule along with others whom I shall choose to help me. For no one man is so wise that he can govern properly alone. He needs the help – the wisdom – of others. In the Land of the East, Seitu and I found peace and joy. It's an open land protected by magnificent mountains. Vote for me and I'll lead you to where we can live without worrying for the morrow.'

There was a murmur when he finished speaking. What that meant he could not tell. It could be a sign of approval; it could also be a sign of disappointment.

Fundi, evidently recovered from the burns he had received two days before, spoke with greater passion and made a highly emotional appeal.

'You don't need a new life. On the contrary, you need to return to the old one. Elect me as your new chief and I'll bring the old life back, even as Mzee Matata intended to do. The gods have been angry with us because we haven't observed the old rites, customs and ceremonies. We must restore human sacrifice. When we sacrificed a male youth and a virgin at each sowing, the land yielded fat crops; the goats, the cattle and the chickens flourished. Only two evenings ago we had our warning. The gods showered us with fire. They did that to show they were disappointed with us. Either we go back to the old ways, the wise and happier ways or we shall be destroyed – our homes and our children and all that we have. There's no escape to a new land. The gods gave Pachanga to our ancestors and here we must live for ever. If we try to settle on a strange land, we shall perish there. Make me your new fetish priest and ruler and I'll restore all the grandeurs of the past.'

Several people shouted slogans as Fundi finished his speech. Leading the cheering were Abedi, Salifu and Zamani who shrieked and clapped their hands with such gusto that others copied them. Fundi had instructed his cronies to shout approval of his speech. They applauded and stamped their feet.

Shabani had been surprised by the reaction of the people to the speeches. It was evident that he had

123

under-estimated the influence of Fundi. He had been convinced that his display of magic in so many ways would prove decisive in the struggle between Ngurumo and Fundi. But he had not reckoned sufficiently with the pull of the past. Nor had he realized the full extent of Fundi's craft and cunning. Fundi was leaning heavily on superstition and on the hard crust of custom. The past had an attraction, perhaps, more powerful than promises that had to be fulfilled.

He rose up and addressed the meeting.

'Having heard your two candidates speak, you can now decide who's to be your leader. Those who wish to have Ngurumo will make this mark on paper.' He drew an X on a sheet of paper and held it up for all to see.

'And those who wish Fundi to be the leader will make this mark.' He drew an O on the paper and held that up.

It was, however, a long time before anyone could make the mark as it was necessary to explain the difference very carefully to every person involved. Then began what was the first exercise in democracy. Shabani sat down and called for a large log with a flat surface which he used as a table. On each side of him sat two youths – a male and a female.

'They'll ensure fair play,' he explained. 'They'll see to it that each person makes only one mark and so has only one vote.'

It was all rather crude, as Shabani well knew, but it was also exciting. He wondered if the people really understood what they were doing. There were moments when he felt sure that, despite all his explanations, the people did not appreciate the significance of their actions.

The voting took a long time. Shabani found himself reflecting that, like so many of the processes of democracy, this was a tedious exercise. Nevertheless, it was claimed to be the best man had yet devised. At least it meant that people decided their own future.

Ngurumo waited for the results in a state of growing anxiety. He knew that much more than the leadership of the people was at stake. His life and that of Seitu would be in danger if he lost. As soon as Shabani had gone, Fundi would use his powers as the new leader to destroy him. That was inevitable. Fundi would always see him as a threat to his authority.

'I'm sure you'll win, my husband,' Seitu assured him, sensing his tension.

'Let's hope that you're right,' Ngurumo said in a manner that showed that he was down-hearted.

Even when all the votes had been cast, they still had to be counted. This took further time, extending Ngurumo's period of suspense and making him so agitated he could not keep still. He found himself envying Shabani's aplomb.

At last, only a short time before the sun set, Shabani called all the people together again.

'You've voted well – for the future. By four hundred and twenty-one votes to two hundred and seventy-nine, you've decided that Ngurumo is to be your new leader.'

A great load rolled from Ngurumo's shoulders. He heard shouts of triumph. Friends surrounded him and hugged him. When the excitement had died down, Shabani joined him.

'Well done,' he congratulated him and they shook hands.

'But have I done well enough?'

'H'mmmm!' Shabani frowned. 'That's certainly a most important point,' he said. 'You mean, do I think Fundi will accept the result?'

'Yes.'

'Come to think of it, I don't.'

'Then it seems that your democracy, as you call it, does not work.'

'It's sometimes in danger of being overthrown.'

'Then what good is it?'

'Don't be impatient,' Shabani pleaded. 'A democracy that's threatened must protect itself.'

'How?'

'I shall have to think about that,' he said.

'How much longer can you stay here, Shabani?'

'Not more than a few days – three at most.'

'Then I shall have to take the people to the new land on my own?'

'Right. D'you feel this will be too much for you?'

'Given sufficient support, I'm sure I can do it, but I fear that Fundi may persuade the people they would prefer to remain here.'

'You can't force them to do what you wish them to do.'

'What are you suggesting?'

'That you take with you only those who wish to go to the new land. The rest can remain here if they don't want to move.'

'That's bad – very bad. It'll mean there'll be two villages instead of one. And then – I suppose the time may come when they won't trust or even endure each other. Then there'll be fighting.'

'You're right,' Shabani agreed. 'This state of affairs

shouldn't be allowed to arise. Persuade all the people to move.'

'But if some of them refuse, what am I to do?'

'Use more than words to persuade them. They've elected you as their ruler and they have to obey you. Let me sleep on this too. Tomorrow I may be able to advise you on what to do.'

'I hope you will,' Ngurumo said and then he yawned. 'It seems that your democracy has its teething troubles and dangers.'

*   *   *

Ngurumo woke up early. He was still worried. Although Fundi had lost the leadership, he would not yield up power easily, especially when he knew he enjoyed substantial support. He was wily and ruthless. He would use whatever means were available to him to take power into his own hands. He would not hesitate to kill if he felt that was the way to achieve his ends.

If Shabani too had spent a sleepless night, he gave no indication of it. He appeared to be as fresh as ever when he woke up that morning.

'I think I've the answer to your problems, Ngurumo,' he said, 'You have supporters. From them organize the most loyal into a body guard.'

'A body guard?'

'Yes. A number of armed men who have the sole duty of protecting you and the rule you stand for.'

If he expected Ngurumo to be pleased with the suggestion, he was disappointed.

'All the men of Pachanga are armed,' Ngurumo answered. 'They all carry spears to guard against attack by wild animals. If I had a special guard, wouldn't they be attacked by Fundi's men?'

'That is something that hadn't occurred to me. We must think again.'

'Yes. Besides, if I'm protected by armed men, the people may not like me or my rule. Or they'll find it difficult to approach me.'

'Then how did Mzee Matata rule without a personal guard?' Shabani asked him.

'Because the people believed he had the support of the gods.'

'Ah, yes, of course,' Shabani exclaimed. 'I should have known this. They believed that the power he had came from the gods and that the gods were all-powerful. He was regarded as being sacred and no one dared to challenge him. This is how men have ruled all over the world from time immemorial. As soon as they lost the protection of the gods and of what was called the divine right, the assassinations began.' He grimaced ruefully. 'Not very long ago, the President of the most powerful nation on earth was assassinated.'

'Didn't he have a personal guard?' Ngurumo wanted to know.

'He certainly had a guard. In fact, it was very strong and well organized.'

'Then it could be the people didn't want him as their ruler.'

'I'm sure most of the people did want him to be their President; he was elected by a large majority of the population.'

'And yet he was murdered. You say there have been many others elected by their people and they too have been murdered?'

'Yes,' Shabani admitted. 'You make me think of things I never thought of before. I'm not a politician.'

'I don't understand what you mean,' Ngurumo chided. 'I want only the best for the people of Pachanga. If they don't move, they'll slowly starve to death. I have to lead them to the new land where they can live and prosper.'

'You know where your people will find life in abundance. It's your duty to lead them there.'

Moments later the people were assembled. Ngurumo addressed them.

'I've called you together to tell you that we're to move to the Land of the East. I've thought much about it and this is the decision I've reached.'

'We're not moving,' Fundi shouted out. He stepped boldly forward. 'Pachanga is sacred to our people. This is the land given to us by the gods of our ancestors. If we desert it we shall die.'

'This can't be,' Ngurumo quickly retorted. 'Seitu and I lived there and we didn't die. We lived well there. We had ample food and so had our domestic animals.'

'That was because the gods were giving you time to return here,' Fundi claimed. 'When you didn't return, the gods commanded Mzee Matata to have you brought down here.'

'And it was here I would have died had Shabani not saved me,' Ngurumo burst out with a sudden passion.

'My friends and I have a proposal to make. We suggest that those who wish to stay here be allowed to do so,' Fundi put forward.

'While those who wish to go, leave. Is that it?' Ngurumo asked.

'Correct.'

'That'll break the tribe and the two factions will soon be making war on one another. If the people of Pachanga are to live and prosper, we should remain one tribe,' Ngurumo said firmly.

The people murmured. Clearly some people agreed with Ngurumo and others with Fundi.

'We're all moving,' Ngurumo reiterated. 'And we start making preparations right away. What is needed now is for a group of men to go to the new site to build houses ready for us to make the move.'

Again chattering and murmuring broke out.

'Listen to me a little more,' Ngurumo called for attention. 'I don't mean to rule alone as did Mzee Matata. I shall choose a number of you to help me to rule and advise me on all matters. I need the wisdom and experience of others. What's more, after I've ruled for fifty moons I shall ask you to elect me again to be your leader. If by then you don't want me, you can choose someone else.'

All these ideas had been given to him by Shabani.

'We must plan our new village so that we can make the best of the land and the space there. To make sure we do all this, the cabinet I shall appoint will decide how our new homes are to be built and how far apart they're to be. I promise you land and a life that'll be better than before.'

It was evident that he had not carried all the people with him. Some of them were gesticulating and talking volubly.

'Listen,' Ngurumo cried out. 'We're only at the beginning of things. Our new friend, Shabani, has told me the people from where he came would be delighted to send others who know much more than we do to help us. They'll teach us how to write and read. They'll show us how to make special buildings in which our children can be taught and learn about the great island of which I'm told we're merely a small part. The men will also tend the sick and make them well again; we'll build a big hut with so many rooms for the purpose. Shabani calls such a place a hospital. They'll bring with them very powerful medicines unknown to us. These medicines can cure those who fall victims to the hot disease which so often kills our people.'

Some of the crowd were impressed by these promises but not all.

'Now,' Ngurumo went on, 'I've appointed Bakari to be my immediate deputy. Other members of the cabinet who will be given special assignments are Ali, Juma, Moshi, Jongo, and Pilipili. They'll sit with me and talk over your problems. They'll help me to decide what's best for us to do.'

The following day, some fifty men with Ngurumo at their head, set out for the Land of the East. Shabani remained behind in the village to instruct the blacksmiths to make tools such as spades, axes and hoes.

Bakari, walking at Ngurumo's side whispered to him, 'There'll be trouble soon.'

'What sort of trouble?' Ngurumo asked.

'Real trouble. I saw Salifu and Abedi creep into Fundi's hut last night. Others went there too. They would only have gone there to plot against you.'

'It seems they're canvassing for support.'

'The old men are particularly unwilling to move. But it's Fundi's cunning I fear.'

'It's that which troubles me, too.'

131

'D'you think you were wise to leave Seitu and your child unprotected in the village while you're away?'

'I haven't left them unprotected. Shabani has promised to keep an eye on them for me.'

'Then they'll be safe. Fundi dares not hurt them while Shabani is there with his magic killing stick.'

12 When the men saw the new land, they were impressed. They had been living in their jungle clearing, in closely crowded huts and narrow lanes, almost in a twilight world. Here, in contrast, was virtually unlimited space. There was brightness everywhere. The blue sky was flecked by a few snow-white clouds.

'We must give ourselves plenty of room,' Ngurumo told them. 'We have to see to it that we all have big gardens and so space the houses that the sun and air can easily reach them. We also have to leave a big space in the centre of the village. That'll serve first as a meeting ground and later as the place where we shall build the special house for the sick and the rooms where we shall learn to read and write. Now, let's put up the houses. We have to move here without delay as the time for the next sowing is getting near. We shall have to till the land ready to plant our seeds.'

The men set to work with a will. They helped Ngurumo to mark out the land for the houses. They cut down trees and lopped the branches. They obtained reeds from the river banks.

In a surprisingly short time, the houses were taking shape. The men sang traditional songs as they worked. They had sensed the immense potentials of the territory. They were encouraged by the obvious richness of the soil. They rested briefly when the sun was at its climax. Then they ate some of the food they had brought with them. They could eat almost at will as fruits grew in abundance in the new land.

The plain was exposed to the full glare of the sun but a cool breeze tempered the heat. This was not the case in Pachanga. There, they were closed in by the surrounding jungle. This prevented free flow of the air. Besides, there was the everlasting torment of flies and other insects.

When the day's work was almost over, Ngurumo called the men together. As they ate their evening meal in the fast failing light, he asked them, 'Tell me, d'you think you'll enjoy living here?'

'Certainly yes,' several of the men answered together.

'Here's a better place, of that I'm sure,' Bakari said.

'Yes, and it can be made far, far better,' Ngurumo added. 'Shabani has told me of places where there's something you can see through the way you can see through water. He calls it glass. He says most of the houses from where he came have this glass. It keeps out the wind and the rain but it admits the sunshine. We can buy the glass if we grow more food. There are places where they don't have enough oranges and bananas and many of the other crops which can easily grow here. The people there will be glad to exchange this wonderful material for our produce.'

'You mean that this glass is like water but that it's hard?' Bakari asked.

'So Shabani says. He tells me, too, that there are places where people many times our number live together. The night is transformed into daylight by something he calls electricity. He says light can be made to glow by someone pressing a switch. The houses and the streets are lit in the same way and there's light practically everywhere.'

'I'm afraid this Shabani is a liar. How are all these possible?' Salifu retorted.

'I don't think he is,' Ngurumo replied. 'The world is full of many things we've not seen or heard of. Don't you remember the great bird-like thing that fell from the sky on to the trees west of Pachanga? Where did that come from? People somewhere know how to fly. They may also know how to make many other things we don't know. Shabani says his people will come to teach us some of them.'

'And then we too can fly,' one man said laughing loudly at the mere idea.

'We may not be able to fly but we'll learn many things that will make our lives better.'

For the second time, Ngurumo sought to know the feeling of the people.

'Tell me,' he said, 'd'you wish to come and live here?'

'Yes, yes,' some of the men cried out again. There were others who were not so sure.

'Mzee Matata said we would anger the gods if we moved out of Pachanga,' one of them said. 'If we make them angry, they'll burn our homes and our crops and destroy us.'

This, Ngurumo saw, was the great problem. Here again was the powerful pull of the past. The people were afraid of offending the gods. They still believed the gods could be treacherous. It had happened – more than once – that storms had ravaged their crops at harvest time. The heavens had opened and rain had fallen as if a great river was falling from the sky; the maize had been beaten and broken and, in some cases, washed away. The showers of fire were also fresh in their minds.

It was the same with many other things. Often it had happened that a child had lived and grown in the womb and then at birth the gods had struck and the child had been born dead. Sometimes people fell from trees, drowned in the river or were devoured by wild animals even though they could climb like monkeys and swim like fish. Who but the gods had slain the children, and taken vengeance on the people – even though it was hard to think of what they had done to displease the gods?

Ngurumo wondered about these things. He had long since concluded that the gods were capricious and malicious. At times he was puzzled to know just what the gods wanted the people to do. If they wished them to remain in Pachanga, why had the gods not provided enough food for them? That was a question which he had asked himself many times and to which he had been unable to find an answer.

The fear of the gods was there. Many people would go to the new land in great fear. It would take them a long time to settle, and if calamity struck, they would say the gods were angry and that he, Ngurumo, had misled them. He was alive to the irony of the situation. If the venture became a success, the gods would be given the credit. If it failed for any reason at all, he would get the blame.

'I believe the gods wish us to come and live here,' he told the men.

It was a bold affirmation but it by no means dispelled the doubts flourishing in the minds of some of them. Although Ngurumo was their new leader, they knew he did not enjoy the protection of the gods as had Mzee Matata. It was not the gods which had appointed him to his position. It was the people themselves. Ngurumo knew they would not hesitate to depose him and perhaps tear him to pieces if they were convinced he had misled them. There was just one comforting thought. Shabani had promised other people would come from Walata to show them how to do many things they could not do now. If that happened Ngurumo felt he would be safe.

When Ngurumo and the men left to return to Pachanga, they had put up enough dwellings to accommodate all the people temporarily. They were satisfied with what had been achieved. It was not a bad start. It suggested what could be done on such a bountiful land in a couple of days.

They made good progress through the jungle. They had with them some of the maize and the fruits Ngurumo and Seitu had grown. These would be evidence of the kindness of the land where the people were to make their new homes. The doubters would be persuaded that the gods were generous over there and therefore wished them to live there.

Before they reached Pachanga Ngurumo learnt that all was far from well. He was met by Moshi, one of his cabinet who had been waiting at the outskirts.

'Ngurumo! terrible things have happened.' He told him in a sorrowful voice, shaking and disturbed.

'What things?' Ngurumo asked.

'Shabani – Shabani is dead.'

For a while Ngurumo was struck dumb. A cold chill ran through his body. He found it impossible to speak. He tried to say something but words failed him.

'Dead! It can't be.'

'Unhappily, he is.'

'How did he die?'

'He was bitten by a python.'

Ngurumo felt the blood drain from his heart. This was tragic. It might well mean the end of all his hopes and dreams.

'Tell me. How did it happen?'

'Zamani asked him to visit her hut to look at one of her children. She said the child was ill. The snake bit him when he went into the hut.'

'What about the child?'

'There was no child there.'

'Then a trap was laid for Shabani. Zamani had the snake concealed in her hut and ready to bite. This isn't her doing alone. Fundi is behind it. This is what he has plotted. I suppose by the time Zamani raised the alarm it was too late to save Shabani.'

'I can't tell, but Ngurumo, there's something else.'

'More bad news? What's it?'

'Your wife, Seitu.'

Fear clutched Ngurumo holding him with such an icy grip that he shuddered visibly.

'She – she's also dead?'

'No, she isn't dead; she has been abducted.'

'To where?'

'That much I don't know, Ngurumo. When light

came this morning she and her child had been kidnapped. They haven't been seen since then.'

'It's Fundi again. Fundi has done this too,' Ngurumo lamented.

'So everyone thinks,' Moshi rejoined.

'Did anyone see anything – my wife being carried away, for instance?'

'No one has said so.'

'Where's Fundi now?'

'He's in the village enjoying the breeze under the large baobab tree.'

Ngurumo ran into Pachanga, his eyes flashing, his manner one of anger and determination. Judging by the way Fundi was sitting, his air so casual and confident, he was expecting Ngurumo's appearance. Ngurumo went up to him.

'Where's my wife?' Ngurumo demanded.

'I haven't seen her. D'you think she's under my smock?' was the sneering reply.

There was laughter from the onlookers at this retort.

'What have you done with her?'

'I've done nothing to her. Haven't I a wife of my own?'

'If you so much as harm a nail on her fingers I'll kill you.' Ngurumo spoke with such an anger he could hardly control himself. The watching crowd became suddenly still.

'How can I harm someone who isn't near me?' Fundi showed no sign of alarm. Although his gaze could not meet Ngurumo's, he held his ground, arms folded, his mouth pursed in a thin line of scorn.

'You know that she has been kidnapped.'

'Everybody knows that.'

'And you know where she is.'

Fundi remained silent and motionless. His eyes betrayed the fact that he was enjoying Ngurumo's torment.

Suddenly Ngurumo grabbed Fundi by the shoulders and began to shake him.

'Tell me where she is, tell me where she is!'

Fundi twisted free of Ngurumo's grip.

'I'll tell you where she is if you'll admit that I'm the rightful leader of the people of Pachanga.'

Ngurumo recoiled from him in revulsion.

'You've taken her away so that you might force me to do what you want.' He spoke with such an unusually loud voice that all around rocked with awe.

'For that I'll kill you.' Ngurumo launched himself at Fundi, held him by the waist and then lifted him into the air with all his strength. The breath went out of Fundi as out of a burst balloon. Fundi tried to thrust his thumbs into Ngurumo's eyes. A lightning jerk of the head saved the eyes. The two grappled together with all their strength, each trying to throw the other to the ground. It was Ngurumo who went down, Fundi on top of him, fingers seeking for a grip of the throat. Ngurumo managed to roll Fundi down over a rugged mass of stones.

Fundi uttered a grunt of pain. Ngurumo leapt to his feet but no quicker than Fundi. Warily, each sought for a hold that would give a decisive advantage. Ngurumo knew that this was a fight in which every stratagem had to be employed. Fundi resorted to butting with the head. The hard skull caught Ngurumo in the stomach, knocking the wind out of him and sending him sprawling. Luckily for him, Fundi was too eager. He jumped to pin Ngurumo down. Ngurumo was still rolling and so Fundi missed the target.

For the next few moments, back on his feet, Ngurumo avoided Fundi while he regained much needed wind. Then he feinted as if intending to strike from the left. Instead, he flung himself straight forward, held Fundi and threw him to the ground. Fundi landed on his back with a bone-jarring thud. His teeth were heard to crack.

Ngurumo gave him no time to recover. He was behind Fundi locking his arms in a way that made him helpless.

'Now, tell me, where is Seitu?' Ngurumo demanded through clenched teeth.

Fundi made no reply. Ngurumo began to push the arms high. Fundi grimaced with pain.

'Tell me where she is,' Ngurumo repeated.

Fundi's face twisted as his agony increased. He was sweating profusely. Still he made no answer.

'Tell me,' Ngurumo urged and then threatened, 'or I'll break your arms.'

'Very well, I'll tell you,' Fundi backed down. 'But first release your hold on me.'

'D'you think I'll fall for a trick like that?'

'Then break my arms but that won't tell you where your wife is.'

'I'll break your neck then.'

'That'll help you even less.'

Ngurumo knew full well that in Fundi there was a ruthless as well as a cunning disposition.

'Swear that you'll tell me where she is if I free you.'

'I swear that gladly.'

Ngurumo felt that he was being tricked but he did

140

not know what else he could do. He loosened his hold. Fundi jumped to his feet. Scowling and massaging the painful parts, Fundi fixed his gaze on Ngurumo. There was black hatred in his eyes.

'I'll tell you where she is only if you'll renounce all claim to leadership of the people.'

'You've stolen my wife to force me to do your will. You'll see what will happen to you,' Ngurumo warned him.

Hearing someone step close behind him he turned to see it was Bakari.

'Ngurumo, this is blackmail,' said Bakari. Ngurumo took no notice.

'Is Seitu still alive?' Ngurumo put to Fundi.

'Yes, she is. At least now.'

'Where is she?'

'I won't tell you now and unless I become the ruler within two days, she'll be dead.'

'Who's holding her?' Ngurumo asked with rage and anxiety.

'She's in the hands of Zamani.'

'Zamani?'

'Yes.'

Ngurumo turned to Bakari.

'Put Fundi in a hut and place a guard on him,' he commanded. 'If anything happens to Seitu, he'll pay with his life.'

Bakari signalled to four men, amongst them Pilipili. They stationed themselves around Fundi.

'Your threat won't open my mouth,' Fundi said wryly. 'I've sworn to become leader of the people or die.'

Ngurumo gestured to Bakari to take Fundi away.

'Come with me. We must see Shabani first.' Ngurumo told Jongo.

He found the body laid in the Hut of the Dead. The snake had bitten him just above the knee. Death, as in all such cases where expert help was not available, had come quickly. The expression on Shabani's face showed that his end had been very painful.

Ngurumo looked sullen as tears began to run down his cheeks.

'He brought knowledge yet they have killed him,' he told Jongo. 'He was tricked to his doom. The snake was waiting for him and no help was given.'

'Who can prove this?'

'The killing was too cunning for anyone to prove it but it was certainly planned.'

'What d'you want to do with the body of Shabani?'

'He must be given a special burial. The wonderful things he brought with him will be kept in remembrance of his visit and the help he gave us in our predicament.'

Ngurumo's thoughts turned to his wife. Shocked as he was by the death of Shabani, the fate of Seitu worried him beyond pain. This was a matter that called for quick but careful action. Had Shabani been alive, he was the one who would have advised him what to do. Now, there was no Shabani. He had to rely on himself.

Along with Jongo, he went in search of Bakari.

'I fear for Seitu. I think she's in grave danger somewhere,' he said sorrowfully.

'That's what I think too,' Bakari said.

'I would prefer to have her back alive than be a ruler. He paused for a moment and then continued,

'This is my decision; I shall yield to Fundi. He shall be allowed to become the ruler.'

'You can't do that. Surely, you must know that if Fundi becomes the fetish priest and ruler, he'll kill you and Seitu. And not only that. He'll kill me and all your friends as well. After what has happened, he won't allow us to live.'

'You're right. But how are we to find Seitu alive before it's too late? Where d'you think she has been hidden?'

'In the caves of the Ancient Dead, is my guess.'

Ngurumo looked startled.

'That's a grim place,' he sighed.

'But it isn't beyond Fundi. I can't think of anywhere else. It can't be in the jungle. Zamani would be in danger there from wild beasts. She hasn't gone to the east; that's where we've come from. Seitu must be a prisoner in the caves.'

'If that's so then more people than Zamani took her there.'

'It has been hinted to me that six men went with them, amongst them Abedi.'

'We must set out for the caves at once. If only Zamani obeys Fundi's command and she doesn't kill Seitu before we get there.'

'You fear that she would?'

'Very much. After all, she has strange and curious urges. Look how she's master of her husband. They say that she does things to him no woman does to a husband; she has made him her slave.'

'There's no time to waste. We must set out for the caves immediately.'

The caves of the Ancient Dead lay a great distance

away, mostly through jungle and swamps. The history of the caves was obscure but they housed many bones and skulls. By word of mouth knowledge of the caves had passed from generation to generation. Even adventurous people went there only rarely. People held the caves in awe and reverence, believing that the bones were those of distant ancestors who had perhaps been buried there when the tribe lived close by. That was before the people had moved to Pachanga and nobody could recall how long ago that was. It could be many moons – nay, many generations.

Reaching the caves would take more than a day. Besides, it was a gamble: no one knew for sure that Seitu had been taken there. Fundi's cunning brain might have thought of some other place. Bakari, Jongo and Ngurumo himself, however, could think of no other possibility.

'It has to be the caves of the Ancient Dead,' Ngurumo told Bakari uncertainly.

'Where else can she be?' asked Bakari.

'I shall go to the caves myself,' Ngurumo said, 'leaving you, Bakari, behind in charge of everything. If Fundi tries to escape, stop him even if you have to kill him. Keep a careful watch. There can be treachery even from those you don't suspect.'

'Don't worry about what will happen here,' Bakari assured him. 'Leave everything to me. Fundi and his clique are in good hands.'

Then began for Ngurumo a nightmare of a journey. With his lieutenant, Jongo, and eleven other men armed with every available weapon, he set out, his heart laden with anxiety. The thought of Seitu in the hands of Zamani filled him with dread. Zamani had always been peculiar and a close associate of Mzee Matata and Fundi. She had been a very willing tool sharing their hatreds and aims.

The journey was arduous. Ngurumo and the men travelled through the heat of the sun. Their path had been little used. They had to make their way pushing through thickets and tangled creepers. They climbed over fallen trees or went round them; sometimes they crept underneath. There were times when the way ahead was so completely barred by shrubs that they had to retrace their steps and take another route. Ngurumo raged inwardly against any delay.

Sweat drenched their bodies. It ran from their foreheads and found its way stingingly into their eyes and down their trunks. When they were panting heavily they paused to regain breath. They did so once by a stream where they quenched their thirst and lay down to rest.

This was how they made their way for more than a day and a half. By the time they were beginning to weaken, they were encouraged by the knowledge that they were close to the caves. At last they came within sight of a rocky cliff tossed up by nature in a convulsion. It had left a high escarpment, riddled with caves at its base. In front of it was a thin line of trees.

With the caves not far away, Ngurumo had the urge to complete the journey. He was in a state of almost unbearable suspense. Suppose he was wrong and Seitu had not been taken to the caves. This thought had plagued him throughout. Repeatedly, he moistened his lips that remained obstinately dry. He sucked in air in harsh little gasps.

The men were very tired but Ngurumo prodded

them on. He led the way with Jongo immediately behind him. He walked cautiously in a crouching position, taking care not to step on any dry twig that would snap and so give warning of their presence.

Ngurumo came to a point from which he could look through the line of trees. What he saw caused his heart to leap in relief. Seitu was tied to a stake driven into the ground. Standing before her was Zamani. Stretched out on the grass were the men who had gone with them. They regarded themselves as quite safe from interruption as their spears had been laid in a heap some distance away from them.

'You're going to die,' Zamani was saying. 'Your husband thought he could outwit Fundi but he was mistaken. He too will be dead by this time. No one can defy the gods of Pachanga and go free.'

She was obviously in a state of high excitement. In her hand she held a thin whip. She raised her hand and struck Seitu with it.

This triggered off all Ngurumo's pent up emotion. Uttering a cry of rage and resentment, he leapt forward. He flung his spear. He aimed more accurately than he had thought. It struck Zamani between the shoulder blades. The impact sent her to the ground with the spearhead buried in her body.

The men who had gone with her sprang to their feet and began to race for their weapons. They were cut off before they could reach them. Outnumbered and unarmed, they surrendered without a fight.

Ngurumo rushed to Seitu.

'Are you hurt?' he asked, cutting her bonds.

'No, my husband.' When he freed her she collapsed into his arms. It was some time before he managed to revive her. By then he had examined her and found no mark or wound.

'You've had a very bad time,' he said, 'but you're safe now. Nothing can hurt you again.'

Ngurumo decided that they could not begin the journey back to Pachanga immediately. They all needed some rest. He was surprised to find how weary he was now that the tension had left him.

'What are we to do with Zamani's body?' Jongo asked.

'Leave it in the caves,' Ngurumo replied. 'That is a fitting place for it.'

The body was left to rot and to lie with a past that had long been forgotten. With his armed men taking turns on guard, four at a time, to make sure that Fundi's men caused no trouble, the rest sank down onto the ground and were soon fast asleep.

On the return journey the following morning, Ngurumo was glad to see that Seitu seemed none the worse for her ordeal. They made good progress. The track left behind when going to the caves made the journey back to Pachanga easier and quicker.

'I've now saved Seitu,' Ngurumo told Jongo, 'but my real problem remains. How am I to deal with Fundi?'

'I don't know.'

'The future of the people still worries me. Fundi is the only stumbling block to progress and prosperity.'

'Truly, he's a nuisance.'

'Fundi won't hesitate to use force to overthrow me. He has already resorted to murder; he plotted Shabani's death. He arranged for Seitu to be kidnapped. I fear he won't give up until either he is dead or I am. We'll have to fight it out to the death.'

Jongo stared at him. 'Yes, that's the answer.' He looked grave. 'But if you lose, Ngurumo . . . ?'

'Then all is lost,' Ngurumo sighed, realizing that Seitu, his child and all his friends and supporters would certainly be killed as well. Fundi would make sure that opposition was crushed.

'Why fight him?' Jongo asked. 'Why not kill him?'

'Murder him, you mean?'

'He's at your mercy. He's unarmed. You've only to bury your spear in his heart.'

It was a suggestion that appealed to Ngurumo. Nevertheless, he shook his head.

'No, I don't want to do that.'

'Why?'

'Because that's the way of the coward. I want to overcome Fundi in a fair fight before all the people.'

Jongo did not agree. 'It's a big risk you're taking.'

'I have to,' Ngurumo insisted.

13 The journey back to Pachanga was arduous. As they neared the village, Jongo asked Ngurumo of the name their new township would take. 'Have you found a name for it?'

'Yes, the cabinet has decided that it's to be called Nyansa.'

'Nyansa,' Jongo repeated. 'It sounds good.' He smiled, pleased with the name.

It was late in the day when they entered the village. The atmosphere of calm indicated to them that everything was normal. First Ngurumo made sure that Seitu was reunited with her child and then he went to see Bakari.

'You found Seitu at the caves of the Ancient Dead?' Bakari inquired. 'And alive and well,' he added with relief.

'We arrived just in time to save her from torture.'

'You look solemn. As your mission was a success, you should look pleased.'

'I would, were my mission completed. But it's not. The hardest and most dangerous part of it is yet to come.'

'What's that, Ngurumo?'

'I must fight and kill Fundi.'

'Fight Fundi? How?' Bakari was shocked.

'With my spear. It's the only way. Come with me. I must see Fundi now.'

They went to the hut where Fundi was being kept a prisoner. When he saw them, he greeted them with an air of defiance.

'You kidnapped my wife,' Ngurumo said furiously. 'You even arranged for her murder. For that you should be thrown to the crocodiles.'

'What has happened to Zamani?' Fundi asked.

'She's dead, as she deserves,' replied Ngurumo warmly.

'Who killed her?'

'What does it matter who killed her?' Ngurumo retorted. 'And tomorrow, one of us will join her.'

'You don't mean it!'

'Tomorrow, after the first meal, we'll fight with

spears. And fight to the death to decide the leadership once and for all.'

Fundi's eyes flickered.

'It will be a fair fight I suppose?'

'Why not, it will be very fair. You shall use your own spear and shield.'

Fundi eyed Ngurumo suspiciously.

'I don't understand you,' he said. 'If you wish to kill me, why d'you give me the chance to kill you?'

'You'll know why when I explain to the people in the morning.'

He turned to Bakari.

'Come, I've no more to say to Fundi now.'

Outside, he instructed Bakari to double the guard on Fundi.

'Now that he can't hold the threat of Seitu's death over me, he may try to escape. Or his admirers may try to help him to escape. We have to make sure he's here in the morning for the fight.'

Ngurumo left to see Seitu and their child. The baby was sleeping peacefully and Seitu was obviously waiting for Ngurumo with some impatience.

'We seem to have been apart for a long time,' she said.

'Well I can't help it.'

'During the walk back from the caves you didn't speak to me.'

'I had much to think about. I still have a lot to think about.'

'But isn't everything all right now?'

'No, tomorrow will decide.'

'What's going to happen?'

'I'll tell you in the morning.'

'You don't want to tell me today?'

'No, Seitu.'

Everything was at stake. The awareness of the fact made him sleepless that night. It was not that he feared death, although that might have filled him with dread; but if Fundi won the fight, all Ngurumo's hopes and dreams would vanish. Ever since he could remember Ngurumo had been stirred and inspired by dreams of a better life. Shabani had told him of many things, some of which he understood only vaguely; others he had not understood at all; but he had grasped some of the possibilities. His people lacked the material to improve the soil, they lacked education to enable the people to read and write; they lacked electricity to turn darkness into day, and they lacked the power to heal diseases and to make life more abundant and prosperous.

Ngurumo wanted all these for his people. Now that Shabani could not tell others of his discovery no one else would come and help the people of Pachanga. They would be lost in the old ways, perishing because they could not throw off their old beliefs.

The next morning, when the people had eaten, Ngurumo had them called together. Fundi was brought to the assembly grounds, guards on either side of him and a supporter carrying his spear and his shield. Satisfied that everyone was present, Ngurumo addressed them.

'Fundi and I are to fight and we're to fight to the death with spears. This isn't a trial of our skill and strength. This is to discover what the gods want us to do. Fundi says that the gods want us to stay here. I say that the gods wish us to go and live in the Land of the East.'

Ngurumo was just playing on the feelings of the people to win their approbation.

'If Fundi is right, he'll kill me with the help of the gods and you'll stay here. If I'm right, I shall live to lead you to the new land. It isn't Fundi who will decide nor is it me; it's the gods of our forefathers. They'll give the victory to the one they favour.'

A loud murmur of agreement emerged as he finished his speech. Many of the people nodded their heads. Ngurumo had shown a subtlety that was equal to Fundi's cunning. The people believed that the gods would preserve the one they supported and that they would destroy the person who was urging the people to do what was against their will. In his heart Ngurumo knew that it was not reliance on any outside forces that would decide his fate and that of the people; it was his own ingenuity, perseverance and stratagem that would count.

Spears and shields at the ready, Ngurumo and Fundi took up their positions. The shields were oval and long and protected most of the body. For some time they sized each other up and neither made a move. The on-lookers were silent and tense knowing that when the fight was finished, one of the warriors would be dead and the fate of the people would have been decided.

It was Fundi who was the first to attack. He darted forward suddenly and launched with his spear. Ngurumo readily parried the blow with his shield. This was how the fight went on for a while, each making a vain attack on the other. Tension mounted. A shout of excitement went up when, in stepping back Ngurumo's heel was caught in a grass tangle; he staggered and almost lost his balance.

Instantly Fundi jumped forward thrusting with his spear. The point cut Ngurumo's upper shield arm slightly. Blood ran down his arm to the ground. The shield fell from his hold. Now he was not protected. Everything was in Fundi's favour. Fundi was quick to see it – too quick. He strode forward, spear upraised. But in his eagerness he forgot to cover his body. As he struck with his spear, Ngurumo jumped aside and at the same time presented his spear. A great gasp went up from the assembled people. Fundi had run on to the point of the spear. He uttered a scream as the poisoned head of the spear buried itself deeply in his chest.

Ngurumo watched with a sense of relief as Fundi fell to the ground. He lay there jerking spasmodically for some moments and then he became still.

'Ngurumo has won!' the crowd shouted. 'Ngurumo has won!'

He was surrounded by a surging, excited crowd all shouting his praises. When finally he could make himself heard, he made a short speech.

'The gods have spoken. They wish you to live in the Land of the East where you'll become the people of Nyansa. This calls for a celebration. As there'll be ample food when we reached Nyansa, we can afford to have a feast here. I order that a feast shall be prepared.'

When the feast was at its climax, Bakari who was sitting on Ngurumo's right hand said, 'You don't look too happy although this should be the greatest day of your life.'

'I'm thinking about Shabani. It's a pity he's not here to see that things have gone the way he wanted. It's a greater pity that he can't tell us more of the things he so often talked about. With his death so much has been lost.'

The festivities continued till late in the night but early the next day everyone set out for Nyansa. Ngurumo led the long column of men, women and children all carrying their most needed household and personal effects. The women strapped their babies to their backs and carried goods on their heads. The aged prodded their weary way aided with long walking sticks while the sick managed somehow tailing the column. Domestic animals were carried in cages, while the few dogs, goats and cows walked alongside the procession.

By nightfall they were in Nyansa. The following day was devoted to building houses and preparing the ground for sowing. Working together on a self-help basis, much was done in a few days. The people were obviously impressed with the new land; some even regretted that they had not moved there before. Soon everybody had settled down.

*   *   *

After twelve moons on the new land, few spoke long-ingly of Pachanga. Nyansa had yielded them abundant food; their cattle, goats and chickens had waxed fat. The well-spaced houses had given them light and air and the sanitation methods suggested by Shabani had proved to be a great blessing. Flies and insects did not trouble them too much; illness and disease were decreasing.

There was a deepening appreciation of what Shabani called democracy. Everyone understood that Ngurumo, their leader, would have to present himself for their approval or disapproval at the end of his term of office. Everyone knew now what was meant by a cabinet. Ngurumo had appointed six men to help him in his administration. Once every moon they met to assess how things were going and to decide what should be done for the good of all.

The cabinet had also made certain laws. These recognized communal ownership of property. No one could take any part of the land and make it his own. It belonged to all the people and it must remain their collective property all the time. The people subscribed to the idea of one man marrying one woman, the pair remaining together until death separated them. The law emphasized that this relationship was not to be weakened.

Ngurumo realized that the people needed to make merry and so he made provision for a number of feasts. They were held to mark sowing and harvesting. On these days there was a great deal of drumming, dancing, singing and merry-making.

In Nyansa, the people had found a land of great promise but Ngurumo was still not satisfied.

'There are so many things we haven't got,' he told his cabinet one day. 'Shabani talked about some of them. It seems people elsewhere are more civilized than we are.'

'What things?' they asked him.

'The thing called education, the thing needed for writing and reading, the thing that carries man quickly over the earth without using his legs, the thing that transforms night into day. And many others.'

'Shabani has been dead a long time and how can we find out about them now?' One of them asked.

'That's true: but there must be a way out.'

His colleagues looked at him like mummies. Sensing their reaction, Ngurumo pointed towards the mountains.

'It was over there – over those mountains – that Shabani came. That means it's the way to the world of wonders.'

'Yes, yes,' the cabinet unanimously agreed.

'I want us to find the way to the outer world and its wonders – the wonders about which Shabani spoke with great enthusiasm. We may not find our way easily but I'm sure we shall succeed. My friends, our greatest days lie ahead.'

THE END

Dar es Salaam,
March 6, 1968.